BADLANDERS

The mining town of Sundown was running into chaos. When the sheriff faltered and shots sounded, hard-case miners took to the streets — fired up and ready for a showdown with anyone who stood in their way. Shane Carson was waiting for them at the jailhouse. Carson was no lawman, but he was a man on a mission — even if that meant standing alone against a murderous rabble. But could anybody hope to stand against such odds and live?

Books by Ben Nicholas
in the Linford Western Library:

THIS MAN KILLS
BLOOD KIN

BEN NICHOLAS

BADLANDERS

Complete and Unabridged

LINFORD
Leicester

First published in Great Britain in 2006 by
Robert Hale Limited
London

First Linford Edition
published 2007
by arrangement with
Robert Hale Limited
London

British Library CIP Data

Nicholas, Ben
    Badlanders.—Large print ed.—
Linford western library
1. Miners—Fiction
2. Western stories
3. Large type books
I. Title
823.9'2 [F]

ISBN 978–1–84617–663–0

Published by
F. A. Thorpe (Publishing)
Anstey, Leicestershire

Set by Words & Graphics Ltd.
Anstey, Leicestershire
Printed and bound in Great Britain by
T. J. International Ltd., Padstow, Cornwall

This book is printed on acid-free paper

1

All Dead at Fable Canyon

The sheriff's seamed face was gray as he sat his saddle watching the buzzards rip apart the human corpses below.

'Executed,' muttered Deputy Cage, sitting his palomino at his superior's side atop the barranca ledge. He pointed. 'See. They were trussed up then gunned down.' He turned his curly head and spat in the hot dust. 'It ain't never gonna end, Marshal, jest keeps gettin' worse.'

'Right,' affirmed the second deputy. 'And look at their rig. Dirt-poor and shiftless. Hell, ain't it ever anybody but the poor that gets it in the neck down here anymore?'

'No mystery about that, boy,' growled the grizzled scout. 'You ever tried to get at a rich man? I knew a feller who tried it once, back once in my younger days. That geezer in question was a total bastard what deserved to die. But this here feller never even got close to him with his shooter on account that high-steppin' breed can afford to be always flanked by flunkies and guntippers you gotta cut your way through before you even get close to — '

'Shut your flapping mouth!'

The sheriff spoke quietly but his tone packed authority. He tried to look away from the scene below but found it impossible. So he heeled his dusty mount forward. 'Get down the mesa slope there and read me some sign, mister!' Whenever Jack Hart called you 'mister', you jumped. It meant the lawman was on a short fuse, which seemed to be mostly the case these days.

Jurd Olan, former West Texas line rider turned scout, put his horse to the steep downward slope and proceeded to descend in a great boil of dust that set the buzzards flapping into the air with hoarse cries of anger and frustration.

A deputy's six-gun thundered and a yellow-beaked scavenger folded up in mid-flight and nose-dived to the rocks one hundred feet below.

Kip Dundas blew gunsmoke from his .45 and grinned proudly.

'Never-miss Dundas — that's what they shoulda christened me, boys. Don't you figger?'

His words were met by silence and the marshal's gray-eyed glitter warned him to shut down and show a little respect.

Which he proceeded to do, although respect would not help the riddled dead. They were strangers to Sundown, nameless foot soldiers in the ever worsening conflict between mine bosses, workers, and just about anyone else with a point of view about 'the troubles' and a Colt .45. They could just as easily have been faceless outlaws from either the 'Scavengers' or 'Raiders': marauder bands which were increasingly threatening the very existence of this most isolated mining territory in Buckhorn County Badlands.

The dead had looked bad from above; they looked pathetically grotesque at close range.

Johnno the hostler suddenly cried:

In solemn light I did survey
A corpse, when the spirit had fled;
In love with the beautiful clay
And longing to lie in its stead!

'Don't start!' snapped Dundas. 'Things are bad enough without us havin' to listen to your Biblebashin'!'

'Everybody shut up!' Hart ordered. 'And the next time you use a gun without getting my OK first, Deputy, I'll wrap it round your skull. Is that clear?' Deputy Dundas nodded and the others fell silent. Nobody spoke until Jurd Olan had completed his survey of the slaughter scene and reported back.

'Killers wore busted boots and spurs but their horses was all shod, Sheriff.'

He juggled some spent cartridges in his hand. 'They were .45s, mostly, one or two .32s mebbe. Seven riders in all. They knew what they were doin'.'

The sheriff nodded. He seriously doubted whether much light would ever be shed on the bloody business that had been conducted here. Maybe, with time to play with, he could have set his deputies to work on the case. But time and manpower were factors he found himself increasingly short of.

'I'll send the undertaker out to collect,' he stated, kneeing his horse into a trot. 'Let's get back.'

'What we gonna do about all this, Marshal?' Dundas called across to him as the party loped along the ravine, heading northwards for the town.

'I'll let you know when I know,' came the sharp reply, which warned against any further talk.

Yet Hart already knew what he would do, what he must do. Had known since the moment he first arrived upon the slaughter scene. The irony in this decision was that the sheriff was aware that, although the plan he now felt compelled to put into operation might well greatly increase his strength in his war against anarchy, it might at the same time cost him more than he could really afford.

Uncertainty camped with the sheriff of Sundown. And none knew better than this twenty-year veteran that this was no way for any frontier lawman to operate.

★ ★ ★

The battered old freight wagon slowed as it rolled noisily into the main street and the athletic figure in blue denim sprang down with his warbag before it could come to a halt.

'Much obliged, old-timer,' Carson yelled with his trademark grin, heaving the bag over a broad shoulder. 'You got me here on time for the stage like you promised. One I owe you.'

'I'd still think twice about headin'

down to Sundown just right now if I was you!' the old wagoner called back. But his passenger was already gone, striding off along the curved main street of Beautel with the jaunty step of someone eager for a party or maybe a free drink or two. There was certainly nothing about the stranger to suggest he might be in any way apprehensive about boarding the first stage the Bromfield Line had found the courage to schedule down to the remote troubled corner of the Big Badlands in two troubled weeks.

'Take caution,' the ancient wagoner called as he clicked the reins, yet he sensed, even as he spoke, that he was wasting good breath. Then he muttered to himself, 'Although I figger if that jasper and bad trouble was to come face to face, trouble'd be the first to blink . . . '

Smart teamster. For it was a fact of life that Trouble with a capital T, and Carson, now breaking into a jog along the street as he glimpsed passengers boarding up ahead at the depot, were old friends.

There was something good about simply watching this man go by, whether he be on the look-out for a pretty woman, a cold beer or maybe a showdown with somebody looking for a ruckus. Well-built, in faded Levis and patch-pocket jacket, he was a man who always appeared to be in an eager hurry on his journey through life, as though charged with more energy than he could ever burn up.

Carson appeared to exude an air of high-voltage energy backed up by a ready grin that likely wouldn't change much whether he was telling a woman he really liked the way she wiggled her hips or was warning some hardcase to back off or start ducking.

But right now, as he weaved nimbly between horsemen, rigs and walkers, the Carson grin was genuine. He needed to get south fast, had been lucky to hitch a ride when his rented horse threw a shoe, was luckier still that he had now reached town just in time to catch the first stage out in thirteen days. He felt A1 and fighting fit — like he always did when beginning a new assignment — so how could he feel anything but good.

He felt even better when he overtook a young woman wearing a travelling-costume who was heading in the same direction, accompanied by a porter carrying her case. He was tempted to slow to her pace, might have done so had he been certain she was making for the depot, or that the driver, already perched up on the box, might not suddenly whip up his team and go highballing off before he could board. He did turn and tip his hat as he passed, almost embarrassingly falling ass over elbow in the process when he got a clear look at her.

For she was stunning. Not just pretty, but beautiful with a heart-shaped face, hair stroked by midnight, and great turquoise-colored eyes that shone.

Was it any wonder a man almost tripped himself up? It was barely a week since his last job in the far north was completed and he had been travelling south most of that time. There'd been barely a moment for him to appreciate the short break from the very different world of his dangerous profession, much less have time for romance of any kind.

Yet he was puzzled when he eventually turned to see that she was indeed following him towards the depot. Why anybody who looked like her might be contemplating the Badlands trail to Sundown this trouble-smoking summer he simply couldn't figure.

Turning to grab a second look back, he almost collided with a stern matron who tsk-tsked at him severely: 'Sir, do you mind? You're not chasing wild cattle along the Cimarron now, don't you know?'

He tipped his hat politely, then raised his warbag above his head to facilitate his progress through the crowd at the landing, caught the eye of the dispatcher wearing the peaked blue cap.

'Room for one more?' he called. 'Sundown.'

'Room for plenty more, sir,' the man grinned, motioning to a porter to take his roll. 'Only two tickets sold so far. This is Mr Fawcett and Mr Grid.'

'Carson,' he said to the farmer and the drummer as they shook hands. 'Great day for travellin', eh?'

'You gotta be crazy, stranger!'

Carson pivoted to see a wizened loser leaning in the doorway of the depot. He had the red nose of a drinker, the bright feral gaze of a rock-lizard.

'Huh?' he grunted.

'Ah, don't pay him any mind,' weighed in Grid, the furniture salesman with spatulate fingers. 'He's just a Nervous Nelly who's all het up on account his brother's drivin' and he reckons we're all goin' to our doom on account of the troubles.'

'And what troubles might that be?' Carson asked with fake innocence, having already been fully and professionally briefed by the ancient wagoner upon the death and devastation racking the Big Badlands.

'Trouble overflowin' down Sundown what's likely just about encircled by bands of hellions — iffen you believe all the talk,' he was told. 'Shootin's, outlaw sightin's and a whole mess of things to keep a man awake at night . . . yessiree,' the lizard supplied. 'On the north side you got the Raiders — throat-slittin' scum, down south there's the Scavengers, mebbe even worse and gittin' stronger every day. And in the middle of it all one hard-lucky town full of drink-crazed miners held together by a handful of lawmen. Rape, robbery and murder — and that's just on the good days, sonny.'

He paused to dab at rheumy eyes with a grubby bandanna.

'Who are they supposed to be murdering?' Carson asked skeptically.

'Anyone they meet, stranger,' the lizard replied. 'They say there's been outlaw packs spotted comin' down from the Kree River country, along with gunplay aplenty in Sundown itself. You name it and most likely it's been goin' on.' He sniffed. 'And now I got me a brother who's got to drive down there that I likely ain't never gonna see again . . . none of you for that matter.'

Carson just chuckled and swung away.

A depot hand tossed up his roll and the runty little driver perched upon the coach roof caught it deftly and stacked it away. He then winked down reassuringly as though guessing what his brother was beefing about. Carson gave him the thumbs up and was buying his ticket from the dispatcher when — there she was again! Miss Beautiful emerging from the press of onlookers, looking as cool as Christmas as the dispatcher deserted him and rushed across to wait on her.

'Board!' a depot hand bawled and Carson went striding forward, reaching for her elbow as she placed one pretty foot on the set of steps.

'Allow me — ' he began, smile fixed in place, ready to dazzle her with his fine manners, when suddenly he was jostled from the side just firmly enough to throw him off balance. 'What?' he grunted in annoyance, then took a second look. Where had this pilgrim sprung from?

The man now assisting the dazzling brunette to board the Concord was tall, broad and expensively dressed. He appeared to be in his mid-thirties with a fine head of prematurely silvered hair which contrasted sharply with deeply bronzed features.

As Carson slowly mounted the steps behind the boarding couple, the girl took her seat and the big man turned to stare squarely at him, eyes ice-green and arrogant under level black brows.

'Yes?' he said in a lofty way, and Carson felt the impact of his personality like a sledge. 'You said something?'

If there was such a thing as hate at first sight it was spawned in that moment as Shane Carson traded stares with a man he had never seen before, but he recognized his breed on sight. High-grader. Too big, polished and rock-solid sure of himself to be anything else. And Carson, the hard man with attitude to burn, was suddenly aware of his own well-worn trail boots and faded denim which contrasted sharply with the fine silk shirt and broadcloth jacket. Plus the joker's good two-inch height advantage over his six feet nothing.

'You jostled me,' he heard himself say, thinking how trivial it sounded, which maybe it was.

'Yeah,' the man said and promptly lowered himself to the seat alongside the young woman.

Fortunately, she seemed to read the threat behind Carson's hard grin. She smiled and said brightly, 'I'm Julia Lee. Mr Mantee just introduced himself, and this is Mr Grid and Mr Fawcett from Arrowhead. We'll all be travelling together so it's best we all know one

another, don't you agree, Mr . . . ?'
Carson let a held breath go. Saved. He
could go off half-cocked at times. He
took her hand and held it to his lips.

'Miss Julia Lee, what a pleasure. I've
already made the acquaintance of Mr
Grid and Mr Fawcett . . . and pleased
to meet you Mr . . . er, what'd you say
you're called, friend?'

'You heard,' said the deep baritone
voice. 'Going far, Julia?'

'All the way to Sundown,' she
replied, looking levelly at Carson as he
sat opposite. 'And you, Mr Carson?'

'Call me Shane,' he insisted. 'It's
Sundown for me too, I'm happy to say.'

'They tell me they're hiring trouble
down there these days,' remarked
Mantee. Their eyes locked. The big man
seemed to have read Carson's brand at
a glance. For he certainly could be
troublesome when it was called for,
sometimes even when it wasn't. That
was how he was made up, and Mantee
certainly wasn't paying any sort of a
compliment.

'I don't understand,' said Julia Lee. 'Hiring trouble?'

'He likely means saloon lizards, miss,' Carson drawled, leaning back. 'You know, smooth geezers in fancy gear who wouldn't work in a fit, so you hire them to mark cards and roll strange dice to trim the suckers. That what you meant, dude?'

It promised to be pretty much like that all the long hot way to Sundown. If they should get that far.

★   ★   ★

No fire. They didn't dare light one out here in the Badlands. There was just the last of the cold rabbit to gnaw on. Failure behind, uncertainty ahead and a blistering afternoon without enough shade to cool a bug burning all around and stretching ahead of a man now.

Seemed a typical scenario this summer for Lobo Quent, Raider leader and fugitive on a cloudless July day as hot as a baker's apron with only hunger, anger and fear to drive him on.

There was a water-hole ahead.

Stubbs said so, and he was the only member of the bunch who'd ever crossed this section of surreal landscape before. Roughly another two miles, the man guessed. Of course, if Stubbs was proved wrong . . .

Quent drew his long-barrelled pistol as his sluggish dun carried his lean frame down one steeply sloped bulge in the dry skin of the Badlands and up another. Gaunted down by weeks on the run, with a five-day growth and ripped holes in his shirt, Lobo Quent was vaguely promising himself to shoot Stubbs down should the compass the ugly runt carried round in his head let him down, but the sober half of his brain knew he would do nothing of the sort.

A man daren't touch off a shot in this country without thinking long and hard about the consequences.

The Raider raised his head as dust rose in sluggish gray clouds from weary hoofs and flies buzzed like demented bees, squinting at the ugliest landscape he'd ever seen.

Beyond a panting ten-mile sweep of yellow sand and cactus, massive primitive mountain ranges raddled by time and the elements brooded above tortured gray hills which lay twisted and ugly like whipped dogs in between lines of jagged-backed canyons that were unchanged since they'd bathed in the blood-red light of a Triassic sun.

Quent couldn't prevent himself from wondering whether they might be out there someplace, even though his party had seen nothing more sinister than a scatter of Indian tracks since crossing into the Badlands from the Breaks three days earlier.

There was no Scavenger sign, yet the mere thought of their ferocious rivals from further south was always enough to set this killer's teeth on edge. But he had to concede that no matter in which direction he looked, crests, hollows, ridges and canyons all lay silent and bleak, the sun-baked flats all desolate and dreary as though they had never known human life and never would.

But Quent was in no way reassured by empty landscapes or singing silence. Nobody had warned him of a possible Scavenger presence this far north, and none in his party had sighted anything even faintly resembling outlaw activity or smoke from a burning wagon rising into a bleached-out skyline.

Yet the killer who'd been reared in Comanche country in the south-west trusted his instincts whenever trouble stirred on the wind. Consequently he planned to fill their canteens at the hole, wait only long enough for his forward scout to return, then push on as hard as spent horses would carry them to put this alien hell behind them.

The water-hole was empty.

The riders sat their saddles in a silent circle round the watering-place which was surrounded by rocks scattered loosely about the base of an ironstone ridge. The heat seemed to sing in the silence. The hole was covered with a gray veil of feathery scum, dry as a spider web. In his eagerness, one of the riders had taken up his canteen and unscrewed it in anticipation. Now he flung it violently at the cliff face and began to curse hysterically until it seemed he was crying.

Quent nodded and a man leaned across from his saddle and smacked the weeper across the back of the head with such force that he went over his horse's head and landed with his boots in the dead gray scum. He began kicking hysterically to fight free from the clinging gray stuff but was too worn-out to be able to keep it up. Panting and pale, he turned his head to stare accusingly up at Stubbs, who in turn hipped round in his saddle to glare at the big horseman behind him.

Suddenly the bunch's weighty trail-blazer found himself the focus of every accusing eye. The man shrugged meaty shoulders and spread pudgy hands. What could he tell them? He'd said the hole was here, and he was right. Had he promised they'd find it brimful with chilled subterranean water? No way. Gently massaging his brow, Quent the killer realized he was beginning to hallucinate. Ghostly desert devils were yapping at him from the ridges. The spirit demons whom the Indians knew well had known the hole was dry and had waited until the band ran itself ragged before moving in for the kill.

He actually raised his weapon again but somehow resisted the urge to empty it at the phantom shapes he imagined up on the yellow ridge, the stable part of his fevered brain telling him these were really not painted Mandan, Pawnee or Comanche but rather fantasies brought on by heat and exhaustion.

In any case, he told himself bitterly, even if the ghosts were flesh-and-blood hostiles, why should he alert the others? The hell with them! They'd had a hundred chances to help him recoup his owlhoot fortunes up north and had blown every one. If every man Jack of them was to wind up pegged out on giant antbeds with their eyelids cut away, they had it coming. Himself? They would never take him alive. Not Lobo Quent.

Then, 'Howdy, pards!' came loud and clear from the throat of the 'slinking redskin assassin' who was magically transformed into the familiar stubble-jawed and buckskin-shirted scout he'd sent off ahead twelve hours earlier.

Quent housed his cutter and stole a sip of whiskey to clear his head and steady the nerves. He appeared every inch the hard leader again as the sunburned rider reined in before him to make his report, which proved good, perhaps even better than that.

Firstly, the man had sighted their back-up bunch on a far horizon several hours earlier, expected them to link up within the next half-day or so, as planned. But the other news was even better.

An hour earlier, the scout had just sighted a stage and six with passengers aboard following the north-south trail through the gullywashes and yellow rock formations some ten miles north-east. Heading their way and kicking up dust. He couldn't believe it.

Nor could Lobo.

'You're just hatchin' a story to get yourself off the hook for findin' nothin'!' he accused, his pistol rising again. Hardship, thirst and a Badlands sun had combined to find, ineluctably, big chinks in the Quent armour, and he was likely going a little loco. 'You're plannin' . . . you're plannin' to lead us on until we drop one by one, then plunder us, while you're the only motherless son of a bitch who knows where the water is!' he accused irrationally.

'Two crew, and passengers packed in tight, I swear to you, boss,' the youthful scout insisted, face pale beneath its alkali coating mask. 'I put the glasses on them. Couldn't count how many there

was. But they got a strongbox . . . and . . . '
Here his face brightened again. 'And somethin' else . . . '

His excitement was unmistakable. Even Quent, teetering on the brink of unreality, caught the quaver in the man's voice. 'Well, what else, you little lyin' shit? What?'

The scout made them wait as he stared from face to face.

Then, breathlessly, 'A woman!'

The silence was total as desperate men, men with possibly only hours to live, men denied all the creature comforts for eight long, hunted weeks, who dreamed every sad night of mountainous breasts and gleaming thighs, stared dumbly at their skinny scout, licking their lips and rubbing their groins, seduced by what they were hearing but deep down unable to truly believe.

A woman on the Badlands Trail?
Impossible!

'She leaned out once,' the scout insisted, spittle running from his loose mouth. 'Ain't jest a woman, boys, but a genuine beauty.'

'How far?' a rider croaked as though in pain.

'An hour north,' they were told. 'And not a mile from here there's a deep rocky basin — '

'Hardrock Basin,' Stubbs identified. 'But what about it?'

'Make an ideal spot to bail up a lousy stage,' the scout insisted, relieved that Lobo had now lost that loco look. 'It'd be a lead-pipe cinch. Wake up, boss! The Lord Jesus does love us after all. Water and dinero, — they wouldn't risk this run if they never had both. Just think, a big pay-load, squad of passengers to plunder — and a goddamn juicy virgin. For the love of God, what more do you want?'

'Mebbe I'll think of somethin' on the way,' Quent replied with a brutal smile, and kicked his protesting mount into a run.

2

Hell Trail South

Dick Grid and Tal Fawcett were fascinated.

When buying tickets for the Bromfield Line's first run south through the Badlands since the bloody troubles erupted several weeks earlier, the farmer and the drummer were solely driven by commercial considerations. They'd expected the journey to prove long, hot and uncomfortable as usual, while the added possibility of danger was surely no added attraction. And even if such drawbacks might be minimized, there remained this particular journey's greatest hazard, boredom.

But this was before they realized it wouldn't be just the two of them making the journey, but instead had found themselves sharing their punishing ride in the kind of company they would have found engrossing anyplace, and doubly so under these unpromising circumstances.

The young woman was responsible. Such refinement, beauty and charm must cause even a storekeeper and a salesman in home and commercial furnishings to feel like eligible young bucks again. And despite the fact both were solid family men, each expected to be at least a little in love with Miss Julia Lee by the time they wheeled into Sundown.

Then there were the men.

It seemed a long, long spell since this region had sighted a stranger of this particular caliber in Sundown, while two of the breed showing up simultaneously had to be a rarity indeed.

Immediately storekeeper and drummer tagged both Shane Carson and Duke Mantee as members of a genuinely rare breed: high-steppers with big guns, men so sure of themselves it made working joes like themselves feel gray and inadequate by comparison.

Not that their fellow travellers weren't friendly enough. Or at least chisel-jawed Carson was, Mantee striking them as more arrogant and aloof. Yet sitting there knees-to-knees with one man who had the easy-grinning, hard-driving look of a man of action, and an even larger, polished version of the same particular breed decked out in rig that might set a working man back three months' wages, would have been engrossing in itself even without the sparks flying between the pair.

Neither passenger understood what had gotten Carson and Mantee off to such a bad start, but it was absorbing to watch and listen as the two settled into a pattern of verbal sniping and verbal point-scoring as they set out to impress the young woman seated between them.

The strange and awful beauty of the Badlands slipped by the windows almost unnoticed, the shocks from the rutted road fortunately largely absorbed by the heavy thoroughbracing of the sturdy New Hampshire coachwork.

'I had my own place in Tragg City, Wyoming,' Mantee boasted as the equipage swung around a high bend, then straightened up over a strip of smooth tableland. 'Saloon, gambling hall . . . ' He arched a black brow at Julia. 'Dancing-girls. Only sizable place in town until — '

'Let me guess,' Carson cut in, a freshly rolled cigarette jutting from between white teeth. 'Until the John Laws closed you down? Right?'

'As I was saying,' the big man went on, 'until I got bored with it all and decided on a change of scenery.' He leaned forward to put a hard eye on Carson. 'Tell me. Have you ever owned anything but a couple of sixguns and a bedroll, drifter?'

'Hey, a man can have a high old time of it with a lot less,' Carson insisted to the girl.

'Sure, shooting people for a living can be a real hoot,' sneered Mantee.

'He seems dead set on convincing these fine folks that I'm some kind of badman gunpacker — ' Carson said evenly, but he was cut off.

'Then you tell us all just what you are, why don't you?' Mantee demanded.

'Simple. I'm a drifter.'

'You certainly don't look like any kind of drifter, Mr Carson,' Julia Lee remarked, studying him keenly.

'Friends call me Shane,' he smiled. 'Well, not totally a drifter, I guess. I work when I need a little money — pretty good at herding cows and lopping trees and such. Occasionally I might sign on with some widow woman trying to run a spread on her own, or even hustle drinks in a saloon. But mostly I just like to drift and have myself a little fun — '

'Or maybe meet up with some fat man with money who wants a business rival shot in the back?' Mantee cut in. 'Yeah, I reckon we read your brand clear enough. Don't we, gentlemen?'

Startled to find themselves drawn into this fascinating exchange, Grid and Fawcett were suddenly speechless. They were absorbed by the conflict but certainly had no wish to become involved, each having come to the same conclusion: that both Carson and Mantee could be dangerous customers best left alone.

They were right on that score. For the simple truth was that Carson was really an enforcer by trade, while in the circles he moved in, Duke Mantee had a reputation every bit as intimidating.

'All right, all right,' Julia Lee said placatingly. 'Enough macho-man talk. Let's talk about what everyone's doing instead. You first, Mr Grid. You're a drummer, I believe?'

Grid was happy to discuss his successes as a toe-in-the-door furniture salesman. Then it was Fawcett's turn, and the cadaverous farmer proved articulate enough to make operating a dry-goods store appear almost exciting, which both he and his audience knew it never could be.

Next came Julia Lee.

She had been engaged to be married

for some time and had eventually made a decision to quit Rapid City and travel down to Sundown where she planned to work while she and her fiancé sorted out a few things and brought their marriage plans forward.

'I guess you're pretty excited about all this?' Carson remarked.

'Of course. What woman wouldn't be?'

'Is he an exciting man?' enquired Mantee in that mocking way he had.

'Certainly.' Julia looked from one to the other and half-smiled. 'Oh, I suppose if I sat Lance between you gentlemen he might appear a little dull and conservative by comparison, but I — '

'Don't have to explain,' Carson interrupted with a smile. 'You folks are in love, and that makes everything else rosy, no matter what. Right?'

'Right . . . ' the girl said slowly. Then she added, 'I guess.'

Carson's brows arched quizzically. But before he could comment, Mantee horned in.

'You guess, girl? Does my sharp ear detect a note of uncertainty?'

Carson scowled. He'd thought the same thing but surely would not have made comment on such brief acquaintance.

'I suppose there's an element of uncertainty in everything people do . . . ' Julia began, gazing out the window at the vast hot spaces of windless air in the still of noon. Then she turned back sharply with a humorless smile. 'No, why should I try and glaze things over? The truth is, I've sensed lately from his letters that Lance appeared to be growing more impatient with our lack of progress, less ardent.' A shrug. 'So I invited myself out to Sundown to see if I might revive his interest.'

Carson sat tugging his lower lip, his expression curious. He had a big hunch that if she was his fiancée she wouldn't have to fret about whether he seemed interested or not.

'He must be loco,' was Mantee's comment.

'Oh, no, he's quite intelligent,' she defended. 'Just a little reserved and conservative, I suppose.'

'Don't downplay dull and conservative,' advised Carson, glancing out the window. 'Over time, you'll find it beats exciting hollow . . . '

The conversation flowed more easily from there and, with the exception of Carson and Mantee, a sense of camaraderie not unusual amongst travellers began to develop as the miles stretched behind them, until they were entering the real Big Badlands regions, all massively awesome and threatening despite billowing white clouds and clear blue skies.

It was a long trip from Arrowhead to Sundown, some sixteen hours in length, and these dangerous days it was executed in one exhausting journey with only a couple of brief stopovers at unmanned stations *en route*.

The undertaking was brutal for both horses and people, yet was not all that unusual in the West, where many long-distance passengers preferred to take their punishment in concentrated doses rather than string it out over a period of days. In any event, that more comfortable option wasn't open to passengers *en route* from Arrowhead to Sundown any longer. A year earlier the line had decided it was too costly and dangerous to support fully manned stations in the Badlands where passengers and crew might overnight, hence the one-day journey became inevitable.

The isolated Sundown region had long been troubled by violence and outlawry, offering, as it did, the desert marauders vast and trackless regions in which to hide out from law, Army or even their own women. That prevailing situation had deteriorated markedly since the big copper-mines and smelters opened at Sundown, attracting all manner of misfits and malcontents until the town had at last found itself obliged to seek the services of a two-gun lawman of the old school to maintain law and order in the town itself, whilst leaving the vast unsettled remainder of the Badlands of Buckhorn County to make out as best it might.

As they travelled, Carson kept leaning from his window to glance upwards at the crew. Eventually and without explanation, he rose, opened the door, stepped out on to the foot-rest, then shut it behind him.

The grizzled gun guard looked down, startled.

'Hey, passengers gotta remain wholly within the coach, mister.'

'What are you two jumpy about?' Carson countered, squinting against the hoof-lifted dust.

'Jumpy?' hollered the reinsman. 'Who's jumpy?'

But they were jumpy right enough, and when they realized he wasn't about to be fobbed off, the gun guard spat a stream of tobacco juice over a teamer's hindquarters and nodded ahead.

'That's Hardrock Basin dead ahead, mister. No way round her, so we go straight through. Ideal spot fer some idjut wearin' a bandanna over his ugly mug to stage an ambush, and it's been tried once or twice recent.'

'Injuns?' yelled Carson against the slipstream.

The driver snorted.

'Heck, mister, the Apache and Navajo got skeered outta the Big Badlands nigh a year ago. That was when this outlaw gang, the Raiders, started aggravatin' us. They still do, but they ain't even the worst of it, nosiree.'

'The Scavengers,' supplied the gun guard. 'You heard of a wolf-pack named that, mister?'

Carson shook his head. He certainly had heard of the Scavenger band during his briefing, but his cover might be called into question were he to admit it. 'You saying you're worried these vermin might give us trouble?' he queried.

'Too far north for them here generally,' supplied the guard, staring at the nearing line of stone hills again.

'But the Raiders? Well, that could be somethin' else.'

Carson shrugged, reefed the door open and rejoined the passengers. He said nothing of his conversation, but from there on in as the walls of Hardrock Basin engulfed them he kept his hand close to his gun butt and his eyes sharp nonetheless.

Trouble exploded without warning.

The coach-and-six was nosing its cautious way through a rock-walled basin with chocolate-colored rock walls rearing high on either side and tight little ravines and canyons cutting away in all directions, when upon rounding a sharp bend in the trail the driver suddenly jumped erect to haul back violently on the ribbons to prevent the teamers crashing into the fallen-boulder barricade blocking the trail.

'Get your hands high or die!' a disembodied voice boomed while the horses were still prancing to a halt. Slowly growing visible were the outlines of the heads and shoulders of armed men rising above the surrounding formations. Mantee whipped out his Remington .44 and fired so swiftly nobody even saw it, not even the alert Carson.

A dusty figure sporting a faded crimson shirt threw up a rifle and tumbled off a high ledge to plummet downslope before hitting hard and coming to rest against a clump of brush, a bloody mess where his face had been.

Carson came clear with both Colts and leapt out on to the trail to land in a low crouch as the coach dragged to a halt, his eyes stabbing for targets as wild cries and curses rising from their surroundings preceded a booming shout: 'Destroy them, Raiders! Just take them any way you can . . . '

The words were swallowed by bellowing gunfire.

'Get them down on the floor and cover them, Mantee!' Carson bawled as he punched two lightning shots at a hat with a head under it. 'Driver, get under the horses and hold them tight from there, and gun guard, do your j — '

His voice was drowned out as the guard cut loose with his shotgun, the big powerful roar of the Greener echoing against the chocolate walls and bringing a piercing shriek of agony in its wake.

By that time Carson was fifty yards away and climbing out of the thick dust carpeting the basin floor, a lithe, swift figure in faded denim with a Colt in each hand and the big grin, the menacing one, locked into place as he went hunting.

This was familiar stuff for a man of the gun who'd traded lead with trouble from Brownsville to Chicago. Shane's first impression was that they were heavily outnumbered, his second and only slightly more reassuring one, that these hellions seemed more desperate than committed, were relying more on sheer firepower than craft and gun skill to carry the day.

A bullet whipped between his legs

and he dived headlong into a clump of brush, then immediately slid behind twin boulders. A volley of rifle fire raked the brush all about him and sent sparks flying from pebbles and outcroppings. In his eagerness, a ragged figure in yellow shirt and red roper's gloves raised his lean body from behind cover to jack a fresh cartridge into his carbine, only to have Carson trigger upwards to smash him backwards with a vicious volley. His Spencer clattering noisily away down the slope, the ambusher tumbled end over end with crimson gushing from the sudden holes in his skull.

Heavy gunfire ringed the coach. Surveying the zone, Carson was surprised to see that the ambushers appeared to be shooting all round the halted vehicle instead of trying to hit it. This seemed loco to him, but only for a moment. Then he felt his scalp pull tight. The woman! They didn't want to kill her. The scum!

Iron-jawed and glitter-eyed, he went stalking.

It was a high risk tactic but he was white-hot mad and this enemy, although numerous, appeared far less committed and dangerous than it might have been. He made two more certain kills plus a possible over the next hair-raising minutes of bloody combat. Until he came close as damnit to stopping the one that mattered most in a furious exchange with a distant black-bearded figure who might well have been the leader.

He found himself a sneak-hole amongst the tall grass and rocks on a hillside where he crouched low to take stock.

They weren't going to make it, he realized. Not as a party leastwise. The odds were too heavy, even if the enemy might lack top-flight gun-savvy and leadership.

He made a lightning assessment. The driver now lay sprawled under broiling sun in the deep yellow dust alongside the Concord with flies buzzing around his bloodied head. Carson sensed the shotgun guard could be wounded, although the man occasionally ventured a shot from beneath the vehicle. But steady and telling sixgun fire kept blasting from the coach itself and he knew it had to be Mantee, acquitting himself every bit as well as he'd expected of someone of that caliber.

The enemy had paid dearly for their attack; but they could afford to lose men while the defenders could not.

To try and drive out of the basin would be suicide; to continue on this way might take longer, but the end results would still be the same. Defeat. Which left . . . what?

By the time he had belly-wriggled back through rocks and brush to reach the coach, the hefty gun guard had been drilled through the heart and had rolled out slowly, dead in the sun. Dick Grid was carrying a light flesh wound but Mantee, Julia and Fawcett all appeared unharmed, as indeed was the

Concord itself, supporting Carson's notion that the hellions wanted the woman alive more than they did a quick victory.

But they wouldn't get Julia Lee while Shane Carson breathed.

He beckoned Mantee to join him, which he did. The pair ducked beneath the coach where they crouched low while heavy bullets thudded into the trail and spanged singing off the surrounding rocks.

'Surrender afore we kill you all!' Carson recognized the voice of the blackbeard he'd duelled with earlier, had heard a henchman call him Lobo. 'You ain't got a prayer and you know it.'

'He's half-right,' Carson panted, noting that his companion, although sweating and intensely alert as he reloaded from his belt, appeared totally cool. Again, he'd expected no less.

Carson talked fast.

Mantee heard him out and stared at him blankly. 'You're loco, drifter. You and me stay put, cover them, the others drive the coach out? What sort of a strategy is that?'

'Have you got a better one?'

'Even if we survived we'd be stuck here without horses or provisions — if we survived.'

Carson's face turned hard as a chunk of Badlands granite.

'What's your better plan, dude? If so, just let me hear it.'

The deep and throaty roar of a high-powered rifle boomed out and the slug bit close to the coach, spattering the crouching figures with stinging shards of gravel. Duke Mantee flicked a chip of split rock off his shoulder and squinted out at their surrounds, his jaw-muscles working and his brows knotted as he probed the veils of dust and gunsmoke with green eyes and felt the sun beating off the earth hotter than God's oven.

Suddenly a thought struck and his broad shoulders slumped a little. He turned to stare into Carson's eyes.

'They want Julia,' he said as though

reluctant to acknowledge the fact. 'That's it, isn't it?' Carson nodded and Mantee groaned. 'And they will get her if we try and shoot it out with these dung-eating lizards, and die . . . '

'You're smarter than you look, dude. But if you mean to make a decision, better make it quick on account we could be running out of time.'

The other glared at him with loathing. 'Of all the cheap trash a man could find himself saddled with for what could easily be his last roll of the dice I had to score you.'

'I like you too. What's your answer?'

'I'm thinking of what my pard Sheriff Jack Hart would do in a situation like this . . . '

The big head nodded sharply in sudden understanding.

'Sure, Hart would do it on account there's no other way. For him or for us.'

Carson stared, trying to conceal his admiration. Mantee appeared to take on a new and larger aura as he added with total assurance:

'What's more, we'll pull it off easy. I've fed tougher men to the cat at my saloon than this bunch of busted-luck scum. Let's hit the bastards with all we've got, and let's do it right.'

'You got a deal!'

★   ★   ★

Lobo Quent swung his shaggy head in an anxious 360° arc around smoke-hazed Hardrock Basin.

'Where the bitch are they?' the outlaw snarled, squinting down at the basin floor from his command post atop a broken-backed ridge. 'They gotta be playin' some kind of game.'

Heads nodded, the ugly and sun-darkened heads of men who fitted into this harsh environment as comfortably as skink or bullsnake. One hardcase was attempting to strap his bullet-shattered arm with his bandanna while another squinted down the gleaming barrel of his rifle at the coach and team below.

The dust was clearing now. Some

time earlier the two defenders whose gunplay had caused such havoc in the outlaw ranks, had suddenly begun circling the trapped stage, dragging their coats to raise thickening billows of fine yellow dust which eventually totally obscured the floor from the ambushers' sight. Ever since the worst of the dust screen had begun to thin there had been no sighting of either man, just the occasional shot coming from the rig itself.

'I don't like it, Lobo,' rumbled a thickset fellow clutching a sawed-off shotgun. 'Could be some tricky play, I'm thinkin'.' The outlaw sleeved his face and continued, 'Mebbe we better just finish it off and get it done. Forget all about the woman.'

Lobo Quent glanced round but saw no sign of support for this proposal in the twisted faces around him. They wanted the woman still, despite their heavy losses. So did he. Less for the pleasure he might find now, but rather to save face and boost morale. Mainly the latter. Without exception, every operation Lobo Quent had bossed recently, during the worst months of his life, had been met with failure, lost men and a diminution of morale until even he'd begun doubting his ability to lift them back to success again.

He needed to get his hands on this woman and the strongbox, and he meant to claim both.

But plainly there must be a change in tactics. And when he proposed a rush on the coach the ready response coming from battle-scarred veterans reaffirmed that they were as committed to their objective as he. It was a heartening thing to see, and Quent was ripping off orders like the Lobo of old as death crept close.

The topographical advantages of a place like Hardrock Basin for bloody ambush were obvious, as had been already demonstrated by the gang's success in bringing the eastbound to a halt. Trouble was, with its maze of fissures, gullies, pits, humps, hills, gulches and thick patches of coarse and concealing Badlands grasses, it also afforded a vast variety of cover for the skilled stalker. Carson and Mantee had not been sighted once since quitting the coach area on the basin floor under cover of their dust screen. But now they could not make it any closer to either the gang-leader's ridge-top position, or the cache of ragged-tailed enemy horses in the gulch in back of the bluff without showing themselves or opening up.

★ ★ ★

Carson nodded to Mantee who instantly slithered away like a prehistoric Badlands reptile. Carson checked both Colts and waited.

Now the sizable party atop the ridge was starting to break up, several beginning to work their way down towards the trail afoot, while others turned in the opposite direction to head down to the horses.

'Better get a hustle on, Mantee,' he breathed.

Eighty yards distant, Mantee was doing just that, moving silently amongst the outlaw horses on his knees, slipping their tethers and unhooking lead ropes as the sound of descending footsteps drew closer.

'Go!' he roared, suddenly exploding to his feet in a giant bound, and a dozen startled broomtails went storming away with tails cocked and eyes rolling. He flung himself behind cover and fanned his right-hand Colt to loose a volley of scything fire into the startled figures upslope.

Lobo Quent was screaming in rage as he started rushing along the comb of the ridge, shouting orders and blasting at nothing — when gunfire erupted on his flank.

Skidding, twisting, yellowed teeth bared in a feral snarl, the killer had but one moment to identify the by now familiar figure of the flint-featured passenger who'd given them most trouble, before .45s flared and he was struck. He fell and rolled behind cover as Mantee came zigzagging up the incline with both guns held at arm's length before him, his Colts delivering a thunderclap of crashing sound honed sharp by dazzling accuracy.

The two-pronged attack was stunning in its ferocity, and as it raged towards its climax, 200 feet below, a trembling Dick Grid whipped up the three-span of horses while Tal Fawcett leaned from a window and scored his first kill of the day when a sombreroed figure in dusty black darted to get out of the way of the rumbling rig and ran right into his bullet.

It was touch and go for the Bromfield coach for some hundred yards or more as it hurtled across the basin floor. But such was the ferocity of the Carson-Mantee onslaught atop the high ridge, along with the hellers' alarm at the setting loose of their ponies, that what was left of Lobo Quent's dog-pack suddenly found themselves scattered, leaderless and indecisive in the face of adversity. That was no way to operate against heavy hitters like Carson and Mantee. But there was a limit to just how far the twin weapons of surprise and superior firepower could take two men who'd already had their share of luck, and Carson delayed only long enough to angle the finishing shot into the downed Quent's ugly skull, and scoop up his double shell belt, before responding to Mantee's shrill whistle from the bluff across the yawning brush gully to his left. Then he was off, covering ground in huge bounds while Mantee laid down a withering cover fire. They convened upgully, where they holstered their shooters and concentrated on speed alone as they headed upwards and eastwards, the sounds of shouting and shooting dimming as they ran.

It was some fifteen minutes or more before two figures, sweat-soaked, rubber-legged and staggering with exhaustion, finally put the basin behind them and lurched onto a huge basalt slab thrusting at the sky.

From the high point the Badlands stretched off into seeming infinity with the strange great headland of Torosillo Sierra massive against the brooding skyline far to the south. Beneath their boots now, the massive pile of ledges, spurs, spires and cavernous depths, strange stones and curious formations were taking on ever changing hues from the blasting sun as titanic sweeps of cloud shadows moved slowly northward before the wind.

The Badlands Trail was a strip of yellow-gray winding its way between nature's barricades. Far out, reassuringly remote, rose a billowing plume of dust, at its base the toylike moving shape of the sturdy green Concord, pride of the stage line.

'Did it!' Carson exulted, slapping his knee with his hat. He turned to Mantee, eager to share the triumph, forgetting for the moment that they were enemies of the kind that were born and not made.

His smile slowly faded; Mantee's features were now stone.

'Better save some of that energy while you've got it,' the bigger man advised harshly. 'By my calculation, we've got forty miles to go afoot without horses, chow or water — and every inch of it through hostile country.'

'Nothing to worry about,' Carson retorted, clapping his hat to his head.

'No?'

'Not compared to our main problem, that is.'

'What would that be?'

Carson shot him a flinty stare. 'One another, of course. Let's hustle.'

3

The Raiders

Nobody really believed it could work but Carson. Yet all agreed to give his plan a try as they suddenly found themselves encircled and surely destined to die if they didn't try something.

From cover, Carson and Mantee squinted up at the cliffs where the sudden appearance of half-concealed figures with guns had caused the southbound stage to halt in its tracks some half-way across the mile-wide basin.

Light glinted on a gun barrel, an accented shout drifted down. 'Surrender or all will die!'

The two traded stares in the shadow of the dark walls, then turned to watch the result as the reinsman, under

Carson's order, began driving the coach in a tight circle around the floor of the basin. Immediately the dust began to climb. Within minutes the entire area was engulfed by vast billowing clouds of bitter gray dust which did not clear for some twenty minutes, when the ambushers descended warily to find the coach-and-six long gone and only two invisible snipers left behind to harry and torment them from cover until darkfall.

★　★　★

Twelve hours later the Raiders' back-up party were still several miles from the agreed rendezvous, still travelling a south-east course away from the outlying settlements they had raided in the north province and making towards their rendezvous point at Niobara Ridge.

They had once been simple illiterate homesteaders but the war had changed all that. The four years of shot and shell had turned the solitary hill people into fighters and nomads and eventually outlaws. Journeying south-east, they were looking for easy pickings but kept look-outs and scouts posted at all times to watch out for the most feared enemy, the denizens of the vast southern outlaw lands known as the Scavengers.

The Scavengers had long been established in the mountains and deserts of the southern regions where they were now enjoying ever increasing power while the less numerous Raiders plundered where they might while casting envious eyes upon their rivals' successes.

Live and let live was the Raiders' sometime motto. But only when it applied to not tangling with the Scavenger clans, and only then when it suited them. Pickings had been lean of late, but should they make it to the Niobora safely they could survive there a spell, where the hunting was plentiful. In the meantime their outriders were up ahead searching the Hardrock Basin region for easy marks, as well as searching for first signs of Lobo Quent. The Badlands they travelled held few fears for them, for what did a nomadic tribe of wilderness veterans have to fear out here where one might ride all day without sighting another human being? Yet the leader's wild daughter was showing small signs of uncertainty as the travois poles cut their deep tracks in the soft soil of this Badlands valley, with the setting sun to their right and with tumbling mile after mile of the same cruel country ahead.

'Why the big scowl, Ruby?' The lean youth riding at her side grinned.

'I smell the stink of something on the wind,' she said fiercely. 'I wish I had one single throat that I might cut it. That might make me feel more at ease.' The boy's grin vanished. He was crazy about the leader's daughter, yet she scared him sometimes.

'You know your trouble?' he grinned. 'Not enough lovin'. Here, gimme a squeeze . . . '

She evaded his grasp and kicked on ahead to crest the hilltop, where she joined Cobweb and Starkey whose ragtag-and-bobtail band of butchers this was. The riders were soon strung out in a long slender line across a vast carpet of reddish-brown grasses and strangely fashioned Badland flowers.

It made a tranquil sight, yet every rider, male or female, toted weapons and travelled fully alert. For this was alien country even to the wide-ranging raiders and stories of clashes and killings between minor bands like themselves had been reaching the north in recent times. Certainly there were sufficient fighting men and sound ponies to deter almost any enemy, yet such was the unnatural atmosphere of this gnarled and silent land that it was still vital to maintain full vigilance until they reached the High Plains and linked up with their forward party.

The girl turned in her saddle as a lithe horseman came out of the brush ahead and rode up to join them. The scout wore a puzzled look as he hipped round in his saddle to stare back the way he had come.

'What is it, fool?' She could talk like that to anyone but the two leaders. Virtually every man in the wolf-pack desired her firm taut body.

'I seen two white men afoot on the wagon trail, Ruby.' He gestured eastward. 'They walk that way, and their boots are breaking.'

'Odd,' she conceded. Then she frowned. 'But why so jumpy? Hadn't you better be reporting to the leaders?'

'These are white men with big shoulders and many weapons,' replied the half-breed. He gestured. 'Men with hard faces. Dangerous. I think we should let them pass on their way . . . I do not feel lucky today.'

'Idiot! They are two and we are many. Go keep an eye on these sons of bitches while I report to the real men in this outfit.'

'It will be done, Ruby.' The scout saluted and heeled away. The girl lashed her mount after the distant leaders, smiling now as if she could already taste the blood.

★ ★ ★

The sun was gone. In the middle distance the sandstone ridges and the cliffs of the labyrinthine valleys and gorges still held the fire of the sun, but here on the low mesa above the terrain was gloomy and gray. Beneath the overhang it was shadowed and still. Carson hunkered down to clean the rabbit he'd brought down with a long shot while Mantee got a fire going.

It was very quiet. Carson scouted for more fuel as the meat began to cook, giving up its juices and filling the night air with its scents. At the base of the lightning-ripped tree there was ample fuel — shattered boughs, dried-out and brittle.

Bellies rumbled.

It was risky lighting a camp-fire in hostile country, but had they bothered to discuss the matter it was certain both would have voted for the cook-up anyway. In the otherworld atmosphere of hostile terrain, it seemed to them that nothing this Badlands night could throw up could be half as threatening as the gun hell they had somehow survived back at the Hardrock Basin.

Carson's daring plan to achieve the escape of the southbound stage from the Raider party in the basin had worked like a charm. But the essential gambit of having Carson and Mantee remain behind to prevent the enemy determining which one of several possible egresses the coach might take from the dust-choked basin — and giving chase — had resulted in a long and bloody clash of arms. At battle's end, the surviving Raiders had taken flight, leaving their vanquishers — or so they hoped — to perish afoot and without water or supplies in hostile country.

But these survivors were resourceful. Afoot, exhausted and mutually hostile admittedly, yet resourceful and as alert as two tomcats taking a midnight short cut home through the dog pound.

But gnawing hunger was becoming a greater problem with every mile.

Twice during the long afternoon they had sighted in the far distance several Raider horses which had broken loose during the siege at the basin, but there was nothing to be gained by giving chase. Each man stoically believed that if they kept to the trail, bagged the odd rabbit, bird or, with any luck, antelope, and managed to find a little water they would make it, although just how far that burg lay to the south was anybody's guess now.

Getting there would still be touch and go, and they were in no shape to go hiving off to chase cayuses that looked every bit as wild as their outlaw owners.

It was significant that neither man shared his thoughts with the other on what they must do to survive. Not they. They were travelling together, but all that that indicated was that each

65

acknowledged it made good sense, not for any other reason.

Eventually they hunkered down to eat on opposite sides of a bright little fire. The meat was good and they tore at it hungrily, ears pricked for every slight sound, their eyes never still. The firelight splashed over them impartially, turning Mantee's prematurely gray hair to gleaming pewter. In the revealing light, Carson for the first time noted how liberally this large smooth-moving man was marked by violence. A small corner of one ear was missing and there was white scarring evident on cheekbone, brow and jaw. His gaze dropped to the bigger man's hands. The scarred knuckles told their own story, a violent one for sure.

'Reckon you might know me next time you see me, drifter?' Mantee growled.

'Huh?'

Then Carson realized that the other was aware of his interest. He took his time prising a chunk of meat from between his big healthy teeth with his tongue, settled back and tugged out his tobacco. His grin was in place as was that smile which could mean anything from 'How about a kiss?' to 'Go for your gun!'

'You've got some-sized chip on your shoulder, haven't you, dude?'

Deep creases showed in Mantee's flat cheeks.

'That could be so, Mr Pot.'

'Mr Pot?'

'Calling the kettle black. You're as proddy as, say, an owlhoot on the run, reckon. Chips on both shoulders the size of railroad ties. That's you, pilgrim.'

'Guess we've more in common than we thought, then.' Carson nodded sagely. 'Uh-huh. Appears like you're going to fit in cozy in a place like Sundown where I hear they would rather fight than eat, I'm thinking. But what's the real attraction there for a dude as full of himself as you in a rough-house noplace like that what's as far away from the bright lights and high times as a man could get and still be in the Territory? Kind of a come-down from bossing a big saloon in a civilized town, I'd hazard?'

'You figure it out,' Mantee said curtly, stretching his powerful body out on the sand, a broken-off chunk of the tree serving for a pillow. 'Anyhow, while we're on occupations, I've finally figured yours.'

'Do tell?' Carson feigned lack of interest. In his job, maintaining his cover was important.

'How many did you cut down back yonder at the basin?'

'Who keeps count?'

'You're a gunslinger. Why don't you admit it?'

Carson's face was a perfect blank.

'You want to take first watch or last?'

'First'll do me.'

They fell silent.

Carson sat cross-legged to check the outlaw's rifle, emptying the piece, reloading, frowning and seeming to concentrate when in reality his thoughts were drifting elsewhere.

He would like to discuss Julia Lee and her chances of survival. But not with this cold bastard. He felt confident the stage would make it all the way through safely to Sundown in light of the good head-start they'd been able to give them. After all, the horses were unscathed and Grid had proved himself a good hand with a gun. Added to this, he and Mantee had cut the Raider ranks brutally. Most anyplace else, all those factors would add up to almost certainty of success. But nothing could ever be bedrock certain in the Badlands. The sky turned a deep, dark blue and the first stars appeared point by point. The nearby ridges were now black, ancient and mysterious. The breeze had turned cold, and it was good.

'I've got a friend in Sundown who might need some help — if you must know.'

He'd thought that Mantee had fallen asleep, now realized he had his hands locked behind his head and was gazing up at the white stars.

'A long-haired friend?' quizzed Carson. 'I mean Jack.'

'Oh yeah, that's right. Your bosom buddy the famous town-tamer and shootist.' Carson grinned sardonically. 'Take a look around, mister. There's no women about to impress now. You don't have to big-note and bullshit to me.'

Mantee appeared to take offence at this. 'And why the hell shouldn't I have a man like that as a pal?'

Carson rippled erect to pace about vigorously as the chill began to bite. 'That lawman has a rep as high as the Rockies, or so I hear. A great rep. What would he be doing with a gun-tipping saloon shark like you for a pard?'

The blaze of Mantee's glare would curl the muzzle hair on a timber-wolf.

'That loose mouth of yours will dig your grave before you're thirty, drifter!' he snarled, then was silent for a moment, fighting for control. For this was a man of titanic furies and bitter enmities, a savage in a silk shirt and fifty-dollar boots. Then he sat up and ran one hand lovingly over that thick silver thatch, seemed to really enjoy what he said next. 'But what would a range-bum gunpacker like you know about real men and real friends, of course. But you can take it as gospel. I was with Jack in Warbow and Canyonville.'

'Both places? Seems kind of odd, doesn't it?'

'What makes you say that?'

Carson shrugged wide shoulders and slid his fingertips under his shell belt.

'Those helltowns are about five hundred miles apart. You'd reckon it would have to be more than just chance that found you at both places together.'

'I run saloons, thinker. I open and close where I please. Figure?'

'And now Sundown. Almost seems when Hart shifts camp you sell up and tag along after him.'

'That's how you might see it.'

'Still seems curious, is all.'

Mantee's powerful features were animated now by a rare kind of intensity.

'Jack is a mighty famous man, as you know. He's the best in his business, which is why they imported him to Sundown when those dumb Cousin Jack miners finally got out of hand and threatened to take over. He's a man with mighty few friends and more enemies than there are flies on a rib-roast. Man like that needs someone he can really count on when the chips are down. Not some half-baked deputy or a dog-pack of lily-livered councillors. A pard with a gun to watch his back is what's required.'

A pause.

'I've saved his life more times than you've got fingers on your right hand.'

Carson clamped his lips tight, jaw muscles working. The temptation to tackle this man in full brag mode was almost overwhelming.

Two things stopped him.

They still had a far piece to travel

together, and it plainly wouldn't make the journey any easier to get to wrangling unnecessarily.

The other reason was that they were being watched.

He'd detected the faintest stir of movement on a rise away to their west, thought it was antelope or perhaps a stray horse at first, then realized it was a figure on horseback, maybe more than one.

'Now just take it easy, hero,' he advised casually, scooping up his rifle. 'But I've a hunch we've attracted company.'

Mantee was a pro. You had to give him that. Instead of jumping up and diving for cover, the big man just yawned and stretched like a man on the verge of nodding off. Then, after a long leisurely moment, he rippled erect, ducked fast behind the lightning-struck tree and had his gun out instantly as though by sleight of hand.

Carson nodded approvingly as he sprang for the cover of an ancient gray boulder close by. He could see nothing above now. At the end of a long silent minute, he raised his head and called 'Better come in. You're making us nervous skulking about up there!'

The two traded looks, silently deciding whether to stay put or go scouting. Then the first ragged gunpacker ghosted out of the darkness, and Mantee swore in shock and alarm.

'More stinking Raiders!' He threw up his shooter. 'All right, freeze it right there and don't touch that weapon.'

'Hold your fire!' Carson barked, feeling his blood run cold as, one after another, more and more menacing shapes emerged.

In that instant the veteran of a thousand dangerous situations realized they'd fallen into error, and it was a big one. They had cut the Raider party to ribbons back at Hardrock, had seen no sign of further danger on their long hike southward.

Now two things were plain. This faction of the enemy had surely sighted them, and had made a complete success of stalking them undetected across their own wild terrain. Now they had them at their mercy.

He could go for his gun and die where he was standing, or he could take a chance on living.

He left the weapon where it was.

'They've got numbers!' he hissed. 'Too many numbers!'

'They're just dumb scum, damn you! But look, that one on the gray is lifting his saddle rifle anyway!'

Whether this was the case or not Carson never knew. The bearded rider was moving however, and suddenly Mantee's pistol stormed. The man cried out in pain and almost toppled from the saddle.

Carson had no desire to be cut to ribbons while he still might have a slim chance to survive. Two lunging strides carried him to Mantee's side to slam the butt of his rifle into his short ribs. Mantee staggered, swore and went wild. Brushing the rifle aside he collected

Carson flush on the jaw with a haymaker that sent him spinning. Recovering his balance, Mantee made to swing his gun upon the ambushers. Carson knocked the weapon down as, from the corners of his eyes, he sighted more and more riders emerging from the floor. 'They've got us outnumbered, you stupid bastard!' he shouted. 'Let's try talking instead of letting them cut us to ribbons!'

The encircling riders appeared menacingly amused by the spectacle before them as Mantee, spitting blood and curses, attacked Carson again with a headlong dive, slamming a knee into his guts as they hit dirt.

'You stupid son of a bitch!' Shane snarled, chopping his fist into a contorted face. 'You lost your mind?'

It seemed not.

In the savagery of the brawl which had the glitter-eyed onlookers smirking with contempt and satisfaction, neither Carson nor the semi-encircling group of Badlanders seemed aware that the bigger man in the brawl was constantly forcing the fight towards the one spot where the camp-ground dipped into darkness, a fissure where the fireglow did not reach.

Only Mantee knew exactly where the hollow of deep shadow lay, only he knew how vital it might prove to be should he play his cards right.

Another tremendous hook sent Carson to his knees. Mantee appeared to dive at him but instead arched over him completely, tucked his head in tight as he struck ground six feet beyond him, somersaulted twice with the fluency of an acrobat, landed on his feet, then dived ahead with a tremendous surge of powerful legs — and vanished.

Instantly the Raiders' mocking delight turned to roars of rage and the night rang to the bellow of rifles and revolvers as they poured murderous fire into the darkness.

There was no response either then or later.

By the time they had brands burning

and had descended into the fissure, a by-now disarmed and bitterly impressed Shane Carson somehow knew his some-time travelling partner had made it.

He swung as someone cursed at him and before he could raise an arm in defence the Badland stars exploded like Roman candles in the sky and he was falling forward on his face.

* * *

He had no sense of time, how long he had been unconscious, how long it was since something had started dragging him along the ground. Spitting dirt and curses, Shane Carson shook his head violently to help jolt his eyes open and found himself lashed by both wrists to a rope that extended forward to the saddle of a big Indian gelding, from where a muscular figure in gray and black twisted round to stare back at him.

'Start runnin' or die, gunpacker — makes no nevermind to me!'

The rope snapped taut and he was hauled over rocks and gravel, arms extended full length, toes ripping furrows. He was still only dimly aware of the indistinct mounted shapes surrounding him as he desperately struggled to get a leg beneath his body in order to heave himself erect.

A rope's end cut across his back and a guttural voice snarled at him. He ignored the pain. If he didn't get upright in a hurry, he realized he wouldn't be able to feel whip, ropes or anything else shortly.

'Loco bastard!' he was muttering as he barely avoided a bushel-sized rock in his path. He meant Mantee, of course. His tone was condemning yet his undertone was laced with something akin to admiration.

Carson had assessed their position at the time of the ambush as hopeless, yet the big man had proved him wrong in spectacular fashion.

But there was some twisted satisfaction in the very fact that, when it came right down to cases, his high-stepping trail partner had in the end proved that he only cared for number one.

He frowned at a thought. He wondered whether Mantee would have acted differently had it been his 'pard', the sheriff of Sundown, in his place here? Correction. He'd only believe that connection when he saw it. Or rather, if . . .

He was suddenly angry now and that set his juices flowing. Angry at the outlaws, Mantee, his situation. He suddenly whipped his legs ahead of his body, dug his boot-heels in deep, then gasped in agony as the rope snapped taut and jerked him upright.

Somehow he managed to retain his footing even as the horseman increased his pace and other riders moved in closer to try and shoulder him off balance.

His rage was strengthening, almost exhilarating. But it couldn't last. After maybe a mile he was forced to fall back on simple willpower to get him through. Never quit. Keep one foot going down ahead of the other. Find the inner core of strength and ignore the outer pain — all through the mind.

The nightmare journey continued for an hour, perhaps longer. Several times he feared he might lose consciousness, so acute was the pain. Then he realized that they were now out in a valley and that the horseman had shortened the length of the lead rope.

'You're gonna pay for all the brothers you accounted for, hot-shot,' he was warned. 'That's after you tell us who the hell you are, what brings you to the Badlands, and who your pard was.' He raised his voice and shouted. 'Ain't that so, pards?'

They were either applauding or dissenting, Carson couldn't tell which. Nor did he much care. One foot after the other. He wouldn't fall and didn't fall until strange shapes rose around him and he realized dimly they were the buffalo-hide shelters of his captors.

And wondered, light-headedly, what

a girl with raven hair and sparkling eyes might be doing at that very moment if she, like himself, were still alive.

★ ★ ★

The sheriff of Sundown was replacing his warrants file on the law office shelves when he saw her emerge from the hotel opposite, pausing to glance both ways before starting across the street.

Jack Hart went totally still for a moment, then dropped his hands from the shelf to tug down his vest and finger the corner of his mustache, his expression a mix of interest and annoyance. He was interested because Julia Lee was such a charmer, irritated because he was anticipating what was bringing her to the office again, and that he would still be unable to help.

None of these thoughts was displayed in his pale, long-boned face as he moved to lean against his sturdy desk. It was a face that had been youthful, handsome and expressive once, but the long years in back of a badge had changed all that. They had coined various nicknames for their town-tamer here in Sundown, as had been the case in the previous towns. The Iceman. Sudden Death. Stone-faced Hart. But of course names meant nothing to him. Only bullets could ever bring him down, folks claimed, although there were new chinks in the armour of the law enforcer if any could ever find them.

Some nights, alone with his thoughts, Jack Hart wondered wearily if he might have extended his stellar career that one step too many.

'Miss Lee, good evening.'

She stood framed in the doorway, studying him quizzically. No sign of her recent ordeal showed in her appearance. The men who had brought her in, the farmer and the drummer, were still recovering at the saloon but the self-assured new arrival was looking as fresh as the new morning, if slightly less agreeable. 'Why, Sheriff Hart, I'm surely surprised to find you still here in your office following our last conversation.'

He motioned her to enter, folded his arms, permitted his face to show nothing. 'If you're referring to today's conversation, which was a repeat of yesterday's and the day before that, then I'm surprised you should expect me to be anywhere else, miss. I made it clear to you then that I would not be leaving town for any reason, and that is how it stands.'

'Not even to perhaps save the life of your best friend?'

'I don't recollect confiding any of my personal affairs to you or anyone else, young lady.'

'Please, don't 'young lady' me, Sheriff. I'm well over twenty-one and you are still on the sunny side of forty, or so Miss Pearl insists.'

That drew a frown.

'You've been discussing me with Ava?'

'In a respectful way. Girl-talk, you

know. I was trying to find out from her why you won't lift a finger to help your friend, Duke Mantee. Or Shane Carson, for that matter. Those men saved our lives in the Badlands, Mr Hart. Surely that is worth something to a peace officer? Any peace officer, even a famous one?'

'Follow me,' he said sternly and led the way out onto the porch.

By night Sundown appeared somewhat better than the raw, plank-and-batten mining-town it really was. There was ample street lighting, while the main street sidewalks were largely illuminated by the saloons and eateries. They saw the lead mules of a freighter swinging wide into the broad street from off the Henderson Road, and they moved back against the wall to avoid the dust.

The mules plodded by with one grimy figure leading them and another following, holding a nodding whip over the team's heads. 'Howdy there, Marshal,' called the cheeky-faced young man atop the load. 'Got yourself a new gal, eh? Hmm, nice.'

'Times like this, this town looks calm as a mill pond, Miss Lee,' Hart stated, hands linked behind his back, ignoring both the salutation and the dust. 'But it can change in an instant into a shooting-gallery patronized by drunken idiots.

'It's capable of making that transformation at any time without warning unless there is someone in this office they fear at least as much as they do death itself. I am that man, and under the terms of my contract I am to remain virtually on duty here twenty-four hours a day to earn the large sums of money I am paid.'

'But your friend — '

'Duke's a mighty capable man, as you may already suspect. As is this fellow Carson, apparently. I'm very sorry, but I'm sure they will manage to survive even if they have to do so unaided by this office.'

'But can't you at least send someone

out to *try* to find them?'

'Miss, some traders of this town recently elected to dispatch an under-manned commercial coach to Wagon Rim through the Badlands, despite ongoing unrest and rumors of various violent incidents which would surely have discouraged more prudent and less avaricious businessmen. The coach was attacked and almost destroyed and good men perished. As result, you'd find both Wagon Rim and Sundown rightly fearful regarding what might be out there in the desert this summer. You couldn't pay men enough to go out there at the moment. And they wouldn't do it for me anyway. They hate me, girl, as my job is to limit their mischief, arrest them where necessary and, yes, kill them when unavoidable. So your admirable inter-cession on your friends' behalf is quite futile. In which case, I bid you good — '

'Good-night to you, Sheriff!' she cried, and hurried off along the plankwalk, high heels tapping, dabbing at her eyes.

The lawman got his hat and walked out to where the dirt of the main street mixed with the rubble of the trail. He stood staring into the huge vault of the northern night sky, shaking his head and muttering; 'You'd better not be dead, Duke. On account of if you are, then my days might be numbered as well. You listening, Duke, or are you past that?'

The only response to come back from the deep night was the hoot of an owl, hunting.

4

Savage Force

His legs ached from feet to hips.

Carson attempted to shift his body into a more comfortable position but the thongs wouldn't permit it. He willed himself to relax, closing his eyes and resting his forehead against the stake they had driven into the earth and to which he had been lashed.

He blanked his mind and rested there in the heart of the outlaws' campground on the banks of a nameless dry watercourse at a spot he calculated to be roughly midway between Arrowhead and Sundown.

No point in fretting over what might befall him. Nor all the things he would miss most if they killed him. Or should that be when?

Treacherously, unwanted emotions

were intruding upon his attempt at meditation. Rage predominated. Rage at Mantee.

OK, so they hadn't been anything like pards and never could be, most likely. But surely there was a basic code that even high-stepping bastards like that were expected to live by?

He conceded that Mantee had had both the initiative and the ability to bust his way loose when they were jumped by the scrofulous Raiders, something he himself had failed to do. Yet he also believed that, had their roles been reversed, and he'd been the one to break free, he would have at least made some attempt to rescue the other.

It seemed now that the coach driver's lizard-faced brother back in Arrowhead had been plainly aware of the increased dangers for the Bromfield Line when predicting he would likely never see any of the southbounders alive again. Carson suddenly grinned toughly, his armour against all adversity. He knew he couldn't blame the coach company.

They had mails to deliver, cash to carry, passengers to cater for and a business to keep afloat. Nobody had held a gun to his hard head and forced him to board. His job down south could have waited until the trails settled down some, he knew.

Then he looked on the bright side. Had he not brushed the warnings aside and jumped aboard that green Concord, he would never have met her.

Even now, he reckoned it had been worth the risk.

He attempted to conjure up Julia Lee's pert all-American features, but was frustrated even in this when a flesh-and-blood face suddenly intruded into his field of vision.

It was the raddled-featured Raider with no chin, holding out something in a bony hand which looked vaguely familiar. An ornate beaded gunbelt. But whose? 'This belonged to my pard Jimmy Bravo what you shot, you motherless bastard!' the hellion accused with venom. He suddenly flung the gunbelt away and snatched a Bowie from his wrist-holster. 'But it ain't all bad. The head man's just give me the go-ahead to pay you out personal. Let's see how much cuttin' you can take afore you start in screamin' like the yeller-gutted nothin' I figure you for.'

This was the signal for a small clutch of ragged-assed hellions and their slatternly women to assemble and chant their hatred at the prisoner, who provoked them even further when he raised his powerful chin defiantly and met every stare with a damn-you-to-hell glare which totally concealed the fact that Shane Carson, drifter, life-lover and man of many secrets, really did not want to die.

Yet he was ready for it.

The way he figured, he'd finally made too many mistakes on one assignment. He wouldn't rate placing his and Mantee's lives in jeopardy to save the people aboard the southbound an error, but their almost casual confidence that they could outfight, outlast and out-smart a vicious enemy sure had error stamped all over it, seen now in retrospect.

So much for second sight.

His time had come — so be it.

He would go out *his* way, standing tall and sassing back.

He grinned so as to enrage his tormentors as he again conjured up the image of the prettiest woman he'd ever seen, made a kind of rough peace with his Maker, decided on playing out one last hunch, then made himself heard above all the shouting and cursing.

'Only thing I'm going to regret when you shove that pig-sticker into me, dogface, is me not being around when all my pards come looking for me when I don't show up down in Sundown!'

His appointed executioner was whetting his blade on a pocket-stone. Yellow eyes narrowed suspiciously. 'What friends?'

'Hell, I reckoned you knew,' Shane responded forcefully. 'Me and Mawby the Scavenger are kin. He loves me.

He's going to go loco when he finds out you've done for me.'

It was a shot in the dark, yet he saw it strike home like a hit to the heart. A score of hits. Every torchlit face momentarily drained of hate, their reaction affording their prisoner the satisfaction of knowing his last shot in life had hit home.

From the outset of this saga with the Raiders he'd sensed that these scum were in reality simply little fringe-dwelling yap-dogs of the desert compared with the southern-based Scavengers. Every pale face before him now confirmed that fact, and he knew this satisfaction would make it just that much easier for him to die.

'You lie!' the knifer screamed when he'd recovered his composure. 'Now I will cut out your lying tongue first, then your heart!'

He charged.

Carson hawked and spat squarely in his face. The Raider sleeved his cheeks and lunged at him with the dancing flames turning the big blade in his hand blood-red.

The man's rage made him clumsy. His knife-stroke missed its mark as Carson swayed back and his momentum brought him within range of the only weapon the bound man could use, his head. It snapped forward at precisely the right moment and made brutal contact to split the Raider's brow from nose to hairline and felled him as though he'd been shot.

For a moment the band of Raiders was stunned, affording their thonged prisoner the 'luxury' of just a few more last thoughts.

He'd lived hard, fast and exciting all his life, believing that he had been blessed with a bottomless well of energy. He had almost — foolishly perhaps — succeeded in convincing himself that he would easily see out five-score years and maybe more. Instead he would die at twenty-seven without wife, child or even a sizable creditor to mourn his passing.

And in his mind's eye he saw a blazing headline ornamenting front pages from the Mexican border to Chicago, where they knew him only too well: CARSON DIES, MANTEE SURVIVES!

'Come on, you bastards!' he roared impatiently. 'Do your worst and damn you all to hell!'

The lean knifer was crippled from pain and loss of blood. Now the leader snatched a burning brand from the fire and passed it to the slatternly woman whose husband had been cut down at Hardrock.

'You got the honor, sister! Avenge your man!'

It was right at that point, as the woman accepted the torch and swung back to Carson with dark eyes blazing maniacally, that a gust of wind fluttered the flame. This caused the woman to flinch away, stumbling a little as she held the brand away from her face, waiting for it to settle some.

It was in the moment when the

flames fluttered, then burned upwards strongly again, that the slow clopping of walking horses sounded and heads swung to see the tall Indian shrouded in a vast buffalo robe come riding from between the lodges leading an unsaddled pony.

'Two Ravens?' challenged a Raider with crossed ammunition bandoleers slung across his brawny chest, for the muffling robes enveloping the rider were immediately identifiable as being of the Kiowa's distinctive pattern. The wearer's physique was upright and arrogantly robust. The Raider frowned as the silent horseman drew closer, still without a word, his face still shadowed by his cowl.

Two Ravens did not reply; in truth, Two Ravens the Kiowa would never speak again, had not spoken for over one hour since stopping to water his horses at a spring, where a Bowie knife came whistling from the shadows to bury itself in his heart.

Now the horseman grunted something

and nodded his covered head. Even a staring Carson suspected nothing until, with a fearsome cry of 'Death to the White-Eyes shall be at my hand!' the big figure leapt from his pony and rushed at him brandishing a knife which slashed at him wildly, missed him by inches but severing the rawhide rope binding him to the stake.

'Use it!' the 'Indian' snarled, thrusting a revolver from his belt into the startled Carson's hands. Carson found himself staring into the powerfully featured face of Duke Mantee in the instant before the big man whirled away to face the bewildered mob.

Reacting in a flash, and faster than he'd ever been, Carson launched into the uncomprehending Raiders. The .45 in his fist opened up at point-blank range like a siege gun, to send bodies reeling away in a shambles of hot crimson. Then his smoking cutter turned upon the leader and killed him with a single bullet to the skull. He felled another two Raiders in quick succession before leaping past their tumbling bodies to spring astride the spare horse as Mantee's twin shooters stormed in murderous support in back of him.

There were fewer than a dozen male Raiders in the camp, and half of these were by now either dead, down or frozen in shock as Mantee filled leather and two desperate men leaned low over their horses' necks and raked horsehide with boot-heels.

Leaning low over his mount's neck with its uncombed mane streaming like the wind in his face, Carson winced as a bullet creased his curved back. But he didn't even glance back as he first jerked a halter rope left to avoid a looming shack, then hard right to go charging past the remuda where tethered ponies reared and snapped their tie-ropes in panic.

A horse was galloping hard behind. If it wasn't Mantee he was in deep trouble, for his gun was now empty. Then came the shout: 'Tight left round that ridge crest, hero!' He realized that his rescuer had also survived the red gauntlet. Somehow he wasn't surprised.

★   ★   ★

The parched creek-bed wound its way back from the long-abandoned change station to lose itself in the humped and eroded hills standing all ghostly in the gray of the false dawn. Somehow at daylight and dusk the Badlands seemed emptier and even more menacing than at other times, a land haunted by the buzzard and the coyote, and more often than not in these murderous times, by human wolves. This was a bleak stretch of no man's land through which the Badlands trail threaded its lonesome way.

Duke Mantee kicked viciously at the rusted iron water-tank, which rang hollowly. The big man turned away, clutching an empty canteen, to glare at Carson who was circling the ruined buildings of the abandoned way station with that familiar quick and springy step, swaggering just a little as any man might to find himself enjoying a dawnlight he'd never expected to see again.

It was several hours since the rescue with still nothing more than a handful of terse words having passed between them. No explanations, apologies or expressions of gratitude thus far. As partnerships went, this one still gave no signs of going very far.

'You won't find water out there!' Mantee was eventually forced to break the silence. He'd counted on there being water at the unmanned station but there plainly was none. Mutual antagonism prevailed, and yet their partnership was surely bearing fruit. Their record now stood at three gun-battles with nothing worse to show for it than a bullet crease across Carson's back. They were free, with any number of dead bodies left in their dust. For two men at odds with one another, they seemed somehow to work together as efficiently as lifelong pards.

Carson remounted and moved off alone to inspect a reach of the main trail. Eventually he drew rein upon finding what he was looking for, namely a patch of dusty road protected from the reach of the Badlands' restless sweeping winds. The wheel and hoof-tracks here were recent, pointing south-west. Following a quick inspection of the sign he nodded and grunted, 'The stage-and-six. They at least made it this far which is just about a guarantee they'd make it all the way.'

It was a tremendous load off his mind and he now felt free to concentrate on lesser matters, such as Mantee and their prospects of survival.

The light was strengthening quickly as he returned to Mantee and his spent horse, which whickered at him in its parched misery. Small wonder the Raiders had not pursued them far, he mused. Those scum plainly knew this country and its water situation better than they.

'Ten miles at tops left in these prads without water,' Mantee assessed. 'We might last another day or two afoot past that.'

'By my calculation that could still leave forty miles to Sundown.'

'We won't make it without water.'

'You knew this could happen when you sprang me, keerect?'

'So?'

'So howcome, damn you?' Carson snapped. 'If you didn't have even water enough for yourself, why in hell did you risk your neck coming back after me?'

He'd managed to contain both curiosity and suspicion until now. He studied the big man, not with gratitude but with suspicion. Sure, he was grateful to be alive. But he certainly wasn't about to trust anyone in this Badlands hell. Mantee tugged a cigar from his chased-silver case, ruefully inventoried what weed remained. He tapped the Cuban on the case, eyes on the trail.

'While I was hiding in the brush at

the water-hole waiting for the owner of these horses to show up and get killed, I overheard a pair of Raider look-outs griping on about just about everything under the sun from saddlesores to who would take over as chief. Then they started talking about the Scavengers . . . ' He paused to light up. Carson was showing a keen interest despite himself.

'Seems that's an outlaw pack with real weight,' he remarked. 'We know for sure the Raiders scum are plenty wary of them.'

The big silver head nodded. Mantee drew breath deeply and exhaled gustily.

'Jack Hart mentioned the pack to me in his last letter. The way those Raiders were talking, these Scavengers are the root of all the big troubles down south.'

Carson waited for the man to go on. He didn't, just puffed his cheroot. Carson felt his anger flare.

'Let me get this straight. You hear a couple of bums talking about the Scavengers, and that was enough for you to risk your hide to bust me loose?'

''Course not. Well, certainly not the main reason, not by a long chalk. You see, I always play the odds, guntoter. So, some time after I busted clear of Hardrock Basin, I got to figuring that the odds of my making Sundown alone and without water in strange country with Injuns and maybe marauders thick on the ground, had to be about zero. I mean, I'm kind of proud of the fact that I'm not a trailsman's bootlace.' He slapped his gun handle. 'I shine with these, yet I could get lost in a big city store. So I figured out a way I might improve my chances — and I was lucky. Your sign from the basin was clear enough for even a city slicker like me to follow.'

Carson's jaw-muscles writhed like worms beneath the taut skin. This arrogant bastard was an enigma. He simply didn't figure like other men. Still, he could now see logic in what Mantee said and in what he'd done. The man had calmly realized he could well die out here alone, had opted to take a huge risk to improve his situation by rescuing Carson in the hope that he could get them through to their destination alive.

'OK, I say we follow the trail but keep well off of it,' Carson stated flatly. 'Maybe if we dodge any further trouble and keep slogging south, we might get to the Overman.'

Mantee, standing with hands on hips as the rising hot wind stirred his silver hair, hooked black brows upwards.

'Overman?' he queried. 'What's that?'

'Old Overman mine. That fat drummer was talking about it on the stage. Arizona. Seems it was the first copper-mine in the region before they opened up big down at Sundown. Been closed down for years. But as I recall there was a town there, which means it might have water.'

'Makes sense. How far, trailblazer?'

'Reckon we'll find that out as we go.'

'You're real grateful I saved your neck, aren't you, mister?' Mantee said sharply. 'Like hell you are!' The big man paused and smoothed down his hair, a familiar gesture. His stare was penetrating. 'I guess gratitude's not your strong point, is it?'

'You're talking about what happened back at the camp?'

'I saved your crummy life, boyo.'

'After you left me for dead at the basin.'

'You still owe me, mister. And I always collect.'

'I owe you for damn near getting me killed.'

In stony silence they mounted up. The sun filled the sky. Thirst raked their throats. As Shane Carson led the way, skirting the stage trail through the grotesque lands, he found it relaxing to focus his thoughts upon the long and far-distant slow rivers, the green hills and the snowy peaks of Wyoming Territory. What the man riding at his side might be thinking was anyone's guess.

5

Buzzard Meat

Seated in a cane-bottomed rocker on the gallery of the Sundown Hotel, Sheriff Hart was taking his first break in yet another twelve-hour day. There were few abroad on the street as yet. It was the early evening hour which separated the heat and hard work of another summer's day from that sunset time when the plankwalks would once again rock to the drum of boot-heels and thirsts would crave and lust would call and the whole seething ritual of a rip-roaring mining-town night would begin all over again.

A prospector with huge bushy beard and cabbage-tree hat went by, nodding his head and saying: 'Evenin', Sheriff sir.'

Hart gave a distant nod, his thoughts

elsewhere. A white-aproned swamper swept down the porch of the saloon opposite in anticipation of the night's business and somewhere along the central block a dog barked and a woman's scream was followed by the familiar tinkle of shattering glass.

The lawman's reaction was to stretch long legs and lean back a little more comfortably. Keen ears detected sounds of petty violence, a domestic row or an altercation between neighbors, maybe. He rarely concerned himself with such trivial matters. He had not been brought in for such duties, didn't care about the traffic, who stole whose dog, which well had been poisoned by whose tomcat falling into it and drowning.

The grizzled peace officer had pinned on the five-pointed star in Sundown specifically to prevent people killing one another and to provide a bulwark between peaceful citizens and those roaring primitives who hacked and hewed at the seams and veins by day and went looking for trouble at night, namely the miners. And he had learned very swiftly always to remain acutely aware of the nomadic bands of hellions who posed an ongoing threat to his town from out there, from the sinister lands beyond the low hills of Sundown.

Despite the corruption, violence and gross venality of the town, Jack Hart believed the most serious threat to Sundown's survival would eventually come from the endless arid lands beyond the city limits.

He forced himself to stretch luxuriously and felt the tension ease from his body. From the dining-room behind him came the musical tinkle of dishes and cutlery, a pleasant, homey sound to the ear of a single man.

His gray gaze followed the undertaker's wife hustling down Broadway with her basket, neat and plump in starched cotton and gingham, her face hidden in a scoop bonnet. For every good wife in Sundown, there were a dozen ladies of the night. The marshal was not disturbed by them either. Such aspects were delicate little water-colors of life in this copper town and he worked on a larger, rougher canvas.

A heavy dray with a cut-under front gear rumbled in off a side street and came towards him. Although he gave no outward sign, Hart tensed a little as the six-mule team hauled its human cargo closer. The voices, rough and loud at first, diminished as a clutch of seamed faces stared at the hotel and the single occupant of the gallery.

Twenty Cousin Jacks *en route* to the night shift out at the Sister Matilda mine. The equipage rolled on by, trailing dust and venom. But it wasn't until it was a block away that a rough voice dared shout: 'Good night, you butcherin' bastard!'

Coarse laughter and derisive hoots erupted and the lawman stared directly ahead. Every first of the month, the Sundown Bank sent a teller round to the jailhouse with an envelope containing 1,000 greenback dollars, the lawman's generous remuneration for keeping in check those men in the wagon and another hundred besides.

He earned every cent — and undertaker, doctor, nurses and apothecary were all doing exceeding well out of his success and the often lethal manner by which it was achieved.

The council had searched far and wide for a man willing and able to keep Sundown on an even keel while the bloated mine bosses made fortunes from their death-trap mines and their golden copper, had considered his fee exorbitant at first, but now saw it as quite moderate.

This would never be a totally safe or half-way respectable town, but it was now possible for decent folk to survive and get on with their lives without the daily risk of being beaten up or worse by great rough oafs who looked like men but acted more like violent children without brains or conscience.

And the harsh reality of the situation here was that those miners, with all their shortcomings and excesses, could at times appear almost innocuous when compared with the human wolves they called the Scavengers and the Raiders.

He heard steps approaching and recognized them instantly. Off came his hat and he was standing erect when the woman mounted the steps and smiled as only she could.

'Hello, Jack, thought I'd find you here.'

He moved quickly to fetch another rocker which Ava Pearl occupied gracefully. She was a tall, feline blonde with dramatic black eyes and mischievous dimples. Until recently the marshal's woman had been the unchallenged belle of Sundown, but now she shared the title with Julia Lee, a fact of life that appeared to worry her not at all.

Little seemed to concern the owner of Ava's Broadway Fashions other than the ongoing challenge of survival in this very masculine and very violent town: not her survival, his.

'I heard them chiaking you, Jack,' she

said, stripping off her gloves and reaching for her bag. She studied him as she took out her cigarettes. 'Are you unmoved or just pretending to be that way?'

Hart's rare smile flashed. Only Ava talked to him like that. Most people treated him with either awe or hatred, depending what side of the law they were aligned with.

'The noisy ones rarely do much harm, honey,' he said. 'It's the quiet and sneaky ones, the loners with bad breath and a twenty-year-old pistol snaked away in the boot-top that you have to watch.'

She did not return his smile. He soon understood why.

'Funny you should mention that, Jack . . . that's the reason I came looking for you.'

He straightened. 'What is it?' Ava was usually quite unflappable, so when she adopted the look she wore now he could be sure it was something serious. She leaned back and exhaled a soft cloud of cigarette smoke, one long leg crossed over the other. 'I was taking coffee with Julia at the Spoon when he came in off the plains. He's not noisy or swaggering, but he does have the look. On him it's as noticeable as I've ever seen it.'

The marshal let a long breath go. 'The look' was a quality peculiar to the genuinely dangerous ones of which they'd encountered quite a few over their years together. It was something which identified a man as trouble. The marshal was disappointed yet hardly surprised.

He'd read something in a science journal once that stated: 'To every action there is an equal and opposite reaction.' This was as true in life as it was in science, he'd found. In relation to his unique kind of work it exhibited itself thus. Whenever some town council, judge, political body, individual or federal office hired Jack Hart and his guns, sooner or later that very action would eventually and almost inevitably result in someone emerging to challenge him. Thus far he'd mainly only had to deal with brawling copperminers, only occasionally came to grips with the desert nomads who would rip your head and use it for a football, given half a chance. He'd cut his eye-teeth as a town-tamer on such people. But there was always the threat of others who, just like himself, largely did their hell-raising and killing with a Colt .45. He said quietly: 'Tell me more about this man.'

★ ★ ★

He was buck-toothed and limber in faded twill coveralls and a battered old hat. His small neat feet were encased in fine bench-made boots of oiled leather, and a scrolled plaited gunbelt encircled slender hips. They'd made a space for him at the bar, for although he was young and didn't look all that much, he had a certain way of carrying himself that was a warning, and there was something about those so-pale eyes that invested him with authority uncommon in any man so young.

And, of course, the gun.

The weapon appeared old and well-used and was carried seemingly casually thrust behind the buckle of a plaited leather belt. It was obvious at a glance that the weapon was well-oiled and in pristine condition, despite its age. Its owner wore gloves as though hefting a shot-glass might prove too rough a task for delicate fingers.

His name was Ellis Ethan and he was searching for a man named Mantee.

'Mantee?' mused the barkeep, scratching his thatch. 'Nope, don't seem to ring a bell, young feller.' The man grinned. 'Why, what's he done?'

Ellis Ethan sipped his sourmash delicately.

'It ain't what he's done but what he aims to do is why I'm here.' He glanced round. The drinkers surrounding him were a mix of towners and miners, some civilized, some who rightly belonged in a cage. 'Big-shouldered gunner man who dresses like a dude,' he announced. 'Thinks he's really somethin', does this geezer. Ring any bells?'

He drew another blank.

A miner said: 'A gunner, you say, feller?'

'Uh huh.' Ethan drained his glass and set it back neatly on the bar. He studied its reflection in the dampness. 'He's makin' thisaway, so I believe. Him and his big old six-shooter gun . . . ' He seemed suddenly to lose interest in the subject as he hitched at his belt. 'How many saloons you got in this pigsty town?' This was provocative talk, yet nobody reacted. The more you saw of Ellis Ethan the more you felt it prudent to keep your mouth shut.

They told him what he wanted to know and he started for the batwings. An avenue opened up for him through the press of people. He had that kind of presence. Intimidating.

Then a drinker called: 'Hey, mister,

did you say Mantee?'

He paused. 'Yeah. Know him?'

'That's the name of the joker who was on the stage with us from Arrowhead nigh a week back,' stated Dick Grid the furniture salesman. 'Saved our lives. Hell of a hand with a gun. Is he a friend of y — '

'Where is he now?' Ethan demanded.

Grid spread his hands.

'Nobody knows. We got separated, so he could be dead by this, what with the Badlands crawlin' with all kinds of bad-asses this summer and all. But tough as teak, he is, so I'm tippin' he's still out there, him and the other joker. Feller name of Carson.'

The young man massaged the back of his slender neck.

'That's gotta be that friend of the sheriff's . . . ' he mused mysteriously. It was as though he gave himself just so much time to consider the subject of Hart, then set it aside. He nodded to the drummer. 'Much obliged. Sounds like I might get to find him out along

the trail somewheres if I went lookin'
. . . and iffen he's still with us, of
course.'

Strong men blinked. Out along the
trail? Hadn't he heard? The trails
surrounding Sundown were reputed to
be crawling with Raiders, Scavengers,
outlaws and God alone knew what else
these days.

'I'd think twice about that if I was
you, son,' somebody advised.

'And then think again,' affirmed
another, a red-faced miner in dusty
gray. 'They're croakin' faster out there
than . . . than they are in these
death-trap mines they make us work in
here.'

This drew some hollow laughter. But
Ellis Ethan just shrugged and started
for the batwings again, before halting in
his tracks.

A tall figure sporting a badge stood in
the entrance-way with his hands resting
on the slatted doors, the eyes in the hat
shadow sweeping the crowd before
coming to rest on the young stranger.

Then the man released the doors which flapped noisily on leather hinges behind him as he came into the room, thumbs hooked behind jacket lapels.

'Mr Ethan?' he said in a voice that carried. 'I am Sheriff Hart. What is your business here?'

'The famous Sheriff Hart?' Ellis's sarcasm was laid on with a trowel. 'Am I supposed to be impressed?'

A vast rustling sound ran through the drinkers and then the saloon was quietening as customers moved back from the two men, thus enabling the marshal to circle the newcomer, his eyes raking him up and down, his hands still hooked in coat lapels.

Twin spots of crimson appeared on the stranger's prominent cheekbones, danger signals for those who knew him.

'I wouldn't do that if I were you,' he warned softly. 'A man might take it the wrong way.'

Hart halted before him. 'Do you wish to leave town of your own accord, or would you rather be thrown out, Mr

Ethan? You see, I am doing a difficult job of work here and your breed invariably complicate it.'

'My breed?' Ethan's' voice sounded breathy and tight.

'Yeah, the gun-punk breed. Well, what's your decision? Hard way or easy?'

'Sic 'im, boy!' bawled a hoarse-throated miner from the back. 'Don't let him do you this way. He ain't nothin' special, but he is a son of a bitch.'

'Take him! Take him!' The miners were suddenly chanting and stamping, their resentment against the lawman visible in every seamed face.

Ellis Ethan seemed to respond, soaking it up as a pulse began to beat in his throat and gloved fingers curled and uncurled at his sides — signs the streetwise marshal read with ease.

The newcomer appeared to be slipping into a crouch when the lawman struck. It was a savage hook to an unprotected jaw that thudded like an axe biting wood. Ethan hit the floor with a crash, and a powerful hand seized hold of his coveralls and dragged him to his feet again, bleeding and dazed.

'If you are smart, which your breed never are,' Hart hissed in his face, 'when you come conscious you'll just keep riding, for if you come back here I'll jail you or kill you, either suits me just fine.' He released the man and stepped back, hands hanging by his sides. 'Of course if you want to take it further here and now we might save ourselves a lot of trouble later on.'

Nobody seemed to breathe as Ethan stood swaying and dribbling crimson. It was plain the man was in no condition to spit, much less gunfight anybody. He was being humiliated in public and appeared ready to weep, but was not given the chance. Hart moved in and swung another brutal punch to the unprotected jaw that drove the man several feet before a press of bodies held him up. Then he slid slowly to the floor, dead to the world.

'Find his horse and take him ten miles towards the Overman. When he comes round he'd better decide it's wiser to go on there for water and keep going, sooner than come back here to possibly get shot.'

Hart was grim as he beckoned the group of miners who'd been baying for his blood moments earlier. The men approached warily. 'It's your job, gentlemen, but you are excused, Blinkhorn.'

Blinkhorn, the ringleader, appeared surprised at his exemption. He had a split second to comprehend the reason before Hart smoothly drew a Colt and slashed him across the face, smashing nose and teeth and causing him to spin fully twice before measuring his length on the floor.

'Next time,' he advised Blinkhorn's stunned friends, 'save your encouragement for someone who's up to a job which not a hundred of your breed have the guts to try together. Well? You're still not moving.'

The Cousin Jacks grabbed Ellis off the floor and moved fast for the doors. They disappeared. The single sound to be heard was the slow thud of the marshal's heels as he followed them out.

'A thousand a month?' an admiring citizen croaked as the batwings flapped to silence. 'That's cheap. He's got to be worth two thousand if he's worth a cent.'

Someone laughed, but many a head nodded sagely. To a stranger, the lawman's actions might have seemed extreme. But this was a town where the law was expected to remain always on top of the heavyweight troublemakers, or the cocky young punks, such as Ellis Ethan. Hart's techniques had worked here before, and few doubted they would work for this strange-seeming gunboy when he recovered from his whipping.

★　★　★

Duke Mantee sucked drily on the neck of his canteen, wiping his stubbled mouth with the back of his hand and glancing sideways at Carson. 'It must be the Overman,' he stated.

Carson looked up from the cigarette he was attempting to roll, the paper rustling in the dry wind. 'Most likely,' he agreed. 'But I still reckon we ought to skirt it.'

The other sounded disgusted. 'Why? Just because we think we might've heard gunplay in the distance last night — '

'We heard it right enough.'

'So?' Mantee gestured at the cluster of buildings crowding the base of the cliff where the land sloped steeply down from their position. 'We are in no man's land in case you haven't noticed. We've been dodging and weaving for days, we've tangled with outlaws and Injuns, have cut tracks all over and sighted riders in the distance twice. We bought ourselves tickets to hell, but now I can see a well down there and what looks like a pump in back of the main mine building. And that is all I can see. No horses, no dust, no sign of life. So I'm going down.'

'It's too quiet.'

Mantee threw up his hands and slapped his thighs. 'It's not enough just to die of thirst, but a man's got to listen to bullcrap. So, damn you, are you coming or not?'

Carson shaped his cigarette into a neat cylinder and ran his tongue along the paper. He deftly rolled the cigarette and thrust it into his mouth. His tongue was swollen and his lips were cracked and dry, but the tobacco taste was still good. He tossed his pouch to Mantee, who was all out of cigars.

'You'll need a smoke if we're going in,' he grunted, which indicated he had decided Mantee's way. Head on down there and maybe get killed, or head off without water and surely die? Not much of a choice really.

He snapped a lucifer on his thumbnail and turned his back to the wind to light his cigarette, eying the Overman over the flame of the match. Although the decision was made, it still didn't set right with him.

They started down, the westering sun casting their elongated shadows across the dry and bitter earth. The wind blew in their bearded, sun-darkened faces and fluttered their shirtsleeves. They looked about as beat as still-mobile men could, yet in each man's gait and in the swing of their long arms there was an evident commonality. At a distance they might have easily been taken for brothers, up close they would simply be revealed as two hard men who didn't know how to quit, who drank from the same chalice of pride and strength.

Approaching a sagging bridge slung over a ravine, Carson slipped his rifle off his shoulder and checked the loads.

'See something?' the other asked.

'Nope. Just mean to be ready if I do.'

'If you do.'

Carson didn't reply. At times their sniping and wrangling had kept him fired up. But not now. There was scarce enough energy to just keep on now without wasting breath.

A creek-bed forked around buildings, dry as dust. A tiny graveyard off to one side had been undercut by the creek leaving a casket exposed.

'You should feel right at home here, gunpacker,' Mantee remarked, indicating the grim sight.

It appeared Mantee still had some ginger left after all. Carson bit back a response and drew ahead to lead the way between a crusher and a huge pile of tailings to enter the compound around which the constructions and gantries had been thrown up.

He started and swung up his rifle at a sudden flurry of movement in the shadows over by the mill. Both stared as the huge turkey-buzzard rose awkwardly and flapped away, its curved beak red as a cardinal's hat.

Then they saw the body.

6

Buck-Toothed Killer

The dead man appeared to be about thirty and was clad in sober brown rig and sturdy boots. He was bearded and wore a colored bandanna wound around his head, gypsy style. There were three bullet holes in the chest and a fourth in the temple. The buzzards had been busy. It was a grisly spectacle, yet for the moment both men were more interested in what lay half-visible beneath the body than the corpse itself.

Mantee made a lunging dive for the canteen but Carson was quicker. He shook it and it gurgled. He deliberately took his time unscrewing the cap before lifting it to his lips. It was heaven. But he didn't take his eyes from Mantee, who stood with feet wide-planted with the gun in his fist angled towards

Carson's legs. Should the man suddenly jerk that muzzle up and trigger, Shane knew he wouldn't stand a chance.

Yet he continued to allow the cool pure water to trickle down his throat and splashed some over his bearded jaw, taunting. Maybe he was a little tetched by heat and thirst. Could be both were, Carson reasoned, which seemed a pretty sound ground for him eventually to hand the canteen across.

Mantee snatched at it with a curse.

Carson inhaled deeply and felt the strength returning to his parched body. He wanted to sing and dance but instead stood perfectly still with only his eyes working, taking in gantries, windlasses, doorways, staircases, rusting machines, apertures, rooftops, passageways.

Rigor mortis hadn't yet set in, telling him the bullet-riddled man at his feet had been alive that morning.

He was puzzled by the headscarf but

it wasn't until he turned the man over and saw the letter S carved into his back that a bell rang.

'Scavenger?' he speculated aloud.

'Looks like this geezer showed up here in a wagon,' remarked Mantee, lowering the canteen and smacking his lips. 'You know — the sign we spotted from up higher?'

Carson rubbed at his eyes.

He prided himself on his eyesight, yet knew he had seen no tracks from above. But as he stared eastwards between high timbered walls now, he could make them out quite clearly at a spot where the earth humped up several feet. The only explanation for his not having noticed before was that he must have been even closer to total collapse than he'd thought.

'Better give me another drink.'

'When I'm through.'

Mantee's rifle jumped up to support his defiance, but equally swift was Carson's six-shooter. For a long, thick moment they seemed closer to gunsmoke than at any time since boarding the stage, which was saying a lot. 'You don't have the guts, Carson!'

'You wouldn't have the balls to shoot a fly off a steak!'

From within a barn adjacent to the main building, something clattered sharply and the tense moment passed. Water and hostilities instantly forgotten, the two fanned out wide like well-drilled foot soldiers before making their way slowly across open space for the barn building, raising no sound from gravel and shale, fingers white-knuckle-tight on sprung triggers.

Their interest in the old mine stemmed from the fact that it stood close by the Sundown stage trail. They were searching for sign to confirm that the Bromfield stage had made it this far safely, perhaps had even stopped over to spell the horses.

When they reached the barn with its battered doors standing open to the weather, Carson advanced to the wall by the doorway. Holding his Colt chest-high in both hands, he gave Mantee the silent nod.

The two plunged lightning-fast through the doorway then dived headlong into the ancient straw, six-guns at the ready and held out before them in both hands.

Emptiness stretched before them.

The big dust-moted cavern of the barn was unoccupied but for a remarkably flashy-looking white pony and four startled saddle-horses.

In silence they rose to check out the animals, searched the saddle-bags. Mantee tugged a sheet of paper from a bag pocket and unfolded it.

It read:

Kill A Scavenger And Earn $20!
Apply With Proof
Sundown Skins and Hides

They traded looks. It appeared possible that this might have been left by a hunter of Scavengers for whom the hunt had gone murderously wrong.

Where were the other riders of these horses?

Mantee moved to a shadowy corner of the building and relieved himself. Carson shaped another cigarette and lighted it. He crossed to an unglazed window to study the main building, which appeared to be a combined bunkhouse, administration center and cookhouse. He sniffed and thought he could smell food. It smelt good.

When Mantee rejoined him they held a parley. There was something mighty strange about the Overman, something they agreed they would be happy to leave that way but for one thing. They still had no way of knowing the fate of the other passengers. They wanted to believe the coach had made it all the way through to Sundown, but it was possible it had got no further than this spot.

'We'll go take a proper look around,' Carson decided, picking up the rifle. For once, Mantee didn't argue.

Clear signs of recent occupation and

violence were evident as they entered the main building, where they were greeted by discarded weapons, over-turned furniture, food scattered on the floor, a man's blood-stained hat.

Upon reaching the next room they paused to listen before going through the doorway together.

A man sat at a table in the corner with his food untouched before him. His head lay on the greasy old table with his hair hanging over his face. One arm hung over the edge of the table and the hand was still locked on to an empty whiskey-glass.

With infinite caution they entered the cooking area to find two more corpses sprawled on the blood-smeared floor with guns in their hands and rifled saddle-bags scattered about the bodies.

In the deepening quiet they stood side by side with ears pricked for the slightest sound. When they eventually heard something it was far from what they expected. From somewhere out-side, perhaps the main front veranda, came the sounds of a harmonica.

They went quickly to the windows overlooking the veranda to see a youthful-looking man in faded coveralls perched on the top step, coaxing a passable version of *Danny Boy* from his harmonica. He wore twin six-guns and had a Winchester .32 leaning against an upright within reach.

He stopped playing but didn't turn his head as he spoke. 'It's all right, gents, I'm done killin' now. Come on out and say howdy.'

They suspected some kind of trickery, so took several minutes to check and double check the surrounds for any others before satisfied that the battered-faced youth — he hardly looked old enough to be called a man — was all alone here with the corpses.

He was making music again when they emerged behind him with their shooters trained on his back.

'On your feet, bucko!' Carson barked.

'Pronto!' affirmed Mantee.

'Whatever you say.' The stranger rose

and turned, pale eyes widening. 'My, my, but ain't you a ringylookin' pair. Sure glad it wasn't you that jumped me when I moseyed in here lookin' for some drinkin' water. Then I'd have really been in deep trouble, I do believe.' A sudden buck-toothed grin broke the homey countenance. 'Ellis Ethan is the handle. Mind tellin' me yours?'

They furnished their names which seemed to mean nothing to the stranger. They then sat him down, without his guns, and demanded to know just who and what Ellis Ethan was, and howcome all the corpses?

'They jumped me soon as I come inside,' he explained, shaking his head as though still astonished by the perfidy of his fellow man. 'Scavenger hunters is what they called themselves. Claimed they were doggin' a sizable party I cut the tracks of on my way up from Sundown. They were chowing down here, and claimed they hadn't eaten under a roof in a week, them havin' been so busy huntin' folks to kill, and all. Then they started accusin' me of bein' a spy for the law and the Rangers who'd been huntin' them all over the desert recent. Next thing, they started roughin' me up and cussin' and all that stuff. Then they told me they were takin' my pony and I could find my way back to Sundown best way I could. And I guess that jest made me mad.'

'And you killed them all?' Mantee prodded.

Ethan's eyes appeared guileless.

'Every dab one, sir. Of course they had it comin', as I'm sure you would agree?'

They looked at one another then back at Ellis Ethan. His face was badly bruised and blackened which appeared to affirm his story, yet it still seemed truly hard to digest.

'One kid carves up four marauders,' muttered Mantee. 'Do you swallow this, Carson?'

Shane was slow in responding,

submitting the young man to a probing survey. 'He could be more than he looks,' was his summation.

'No, I reckon he's less. It's my guess he suckered those scum in somehow, then backshot them without warning. That geezer killed at his chow sure wasn't expecting a bullet in the back.'

'What do you say to that, kid?' Carson asked.

'Only that I always tell the truth, sir.'

It was difficult to resist the candour of those pale young eyes. They might have deliberated longer and questioned him further but for the fact that the sight and smell of food was virtually impossible for half-starved men to resist, so eventually they relaxed a little and settled down to attack the left-over chow the Scavenger-hunters wouldn't be needing any more.

Even so, they kept glancing curiously across at the young man seated, relaxed, in a broken chair, twiddling his thumbs and looking both at ease and innocent. They were wondering just what he might really know, what he'd possibly done, what he could be thinking.

Mainly what Ellis Ethan was thinking at that moment was that he had to be about the luckiest killer in the Badlands — as well as one of the best informed. For he knew that the taller of these big men seated across from him now was a close associate of the lawman who'd recently beat up on him, then posted him from Sundown.

He'd almost ruined everything by visiting Sundown, he mused. He had a job to do, which was to travel uptrail in search of a possible government agent rumored to be coming to town.

He'd been diverted to Sundown by news that a pair of newcomers who looked like gunfighters had arrived. The name and reputation of Duke Mantee rang a bell and he had foolishly gone looking for the big rep, who'd gotten the jump on him and then the sheriff had kicked him out of town.

He'd reached the station here battered, bruised and in a lethal temper, where he was again tempted by fate, this time by the presence of a bunch of Scavenger-hunters.

His Scavenger blood boiled.

No errors this time. He'd gunned them all and some time later had seen Mantee walk in with another, possibly some kind of law. The certainty was that both would have to prove to be anti-Scavenger, and he would be a hero of the stronghold when he brought home their dirty scalps.

His father would be proud. His father was second in command of the outlaw clan. So the lethal young man sat with hammering heart, realizing that the hour he'd been waiting for all his life, that opportunity which would catapult him from the upper echelons of the tribe into the star status of the Hickoks, Earps and the Bonneys appeared suddenly and unexpectedly to be close at hand.

While Carson and Mantee continued eating and soaking up cold well-water, Ethan spent his time cleaning his guns.

7

Notch-Cutter

'Miss!' the miner called from the doorway. 'Miller's started in coughin' again.'

'All right, I'm coming, Abel,' Ava Pearl replied, gathering up her things. 'Julia, would you like to lend a hand?'

'That's what I'm here for, isn't it?'

They quit the room together with Julia clutching the lamp and Ava the medications. Shadows swung and tilted in the hallway as the young women hurried along to the room where the miner injured in the last rock fall lay on a high cot, coughing rackingly.

The four-bed hospital off Broadway was Ava's part-time interest and had become Julia's also. They tended the sick man for some time, finally left him sedated and sleeping. Upon returning to the reception area they found it crowded with four burly miners supporting a fifth who was nursing a broken arm. 'Another accident, Mr Fort?' Ava asked as they guided the injured man to a chair.

'Yeah, Miss Pearl,' big-boned Holte Fort replied darkly. 'Hart accidentally hit him with a gunbarrel and busted the bone.'

The women exchanged silent glances. They then did what they could for the injured man until the doctor came through from another room to take over. Three miners left but Fort remained. 'Never meant to talk smart that way, Miss Pearl,' he apologized. 'You been a real angel to us, you too, Miss Lee. But that danged sheriff — '

'Is simply doing his job,' Ava finished for him. 'Is there anything else, Mr Fort?'

'Just wondered if there's any news on them fellers from off of your stage, Miss Lee? You know? The ones you had to leave behind up north.'

'Not that I've heard,' replied Julia.

The man flushed a little. 'Er, I guess you'll be leavin' any day now to get married then, huh? Leastways so everybody says.'

'Why, I'm afraid not,' Julia admitted. She looked at Ava. 'Lance wired me from the West to explain why he wasn't here to meet me. He grew tired of waiting and has officially called off the wedding.'

'Oh, honey, I'm so sorry,' Ava said, going to her and placing an arm around her shoulders. 'Men!'

'Heck, they ain't all no-account, ladies.'

The women broke apart, realizing that Fort was still standing there. They looked at him inquiringly. He appeared almost happy in a hard-faced kind of way, despite the fact that he had a reputation as the most violent miner in town and leader of its most troublesome faction.

'You're a right handsome woman, Miss Julia,' he said, going to the door.

'Reckon you won't have no trouble at all findin' a beau here in Sundown iffen you was to elect to stay on.'

'My glory, Julia!' Ava gasped as he went out. 'I do believe he means himself.' She was right. The pretty newcomer's presence at the hospital had roused unfamiliar feelings in Fort's brawny breast. But such sentiments were swiftly set aside when, after walking two blocks down Broadway, his outsized figure swung down an alley to reach a low dive filled with miners drinking wine and debating the latest violent incident involving a miner and the sheriff, their natural enemy.

There had been previous heated meetings such as this since Hart's hiring, many such. Some had been orderly enough, others furiously heated and marked by brawling and raging protests against the council's action in importing a man of the gun like Jack Hart to deal with them, as if they were outlaws or savages. But tonight's gathering was different, a little quieter on the surface than usual, yet somehow far more menacing. During his long months on the streets, Sheriff Hart had meted out much harsher treatment to brawling rioters than today's busted arm for the miner at the hospital. But it was the timing of this latest incident that was significant, as it represented the first lawman-miner clash since Fort and his turbulent fellow-Cousin Jacks had learned of a man named Mantee having been aboard the Arrowhead stage when it was attacked way up at Hardrock Basin.

There was a miner from the Copper King who'd been living at Warbow when Jack Hart was brought in to subdue the wild cowboys of the trail crews the previous year. During the sheriff's tenure, his friend Duke Mantee had arrived to take over a saloon there. Subsequently the big man had seemed to fill the role as unofficial deputy and back-up whenever Hart found himself having difficulties with the wild riders.

As far as both this man and Holte

Fort were concerned, the news that Mantee had been *en route* to Sundown from the north could mean only one thing. Namely that Hart was once again bringing in an ally to a town under his control who was known to be a lethal hand with the guns, to back his play here again. In Sundown and against them. Two bloody gunfighters instead of just the one! Ironically, it now appeared that Mantee's attempt to rejoin Hart here might well have already cost him his life, considering the man's circumstances when last sighted. But now that apppeared almost incidental in the eyes of the half-wild Cousin Jacks. All that that signified for them was that Hart, already notorious for the ruthlessness of his law enforcement, was in fact breaking the law they were expected to respect by importing another gunman — a killer maybe to back his play upon the streets of Sundown.

Their streets!

Fort interpreted this as the final

straw, the ultimate challenge to their rights to be treated as free American citizens, not some breed of primitives to be juggled, beaten and shot at will by a gunfighter sporting a lawman's badge. 'We knew we could never trust that badge-toter to lie straight in bed!' Fort mouthed, fingering an old scar on his brawny forehead, a legacy of a clash with the law which had landed him first in Ava's clinic, then the jailhouse. His fist smashed a table. 'Three deputies — yet he still wants more muscle. Goddamn — '

'But what if this Mantee guy's been chewed up by the Raiders or mebbe even the Scavengers, Holte?' a husky brute slurred.

'The hell with them Scavengers!' Fort snorted. 'All we hear these days is that those bastards have been lurking around hereabouts waitin' for the right time to wipe this town offen the map and ride off with all our copper, gold and money.'

He gestured violently.

'Where are they? Seems there ain't nobody seen 'em about for certain sure. Could be just all jaw and bull-dust. But Hart is real, and ever since learnin' this pard of his'n is on his way, I for one have known we either got to take the bull by the horns and strike back or just agree that we're gonna lie down and end up as beat-up and downtrodden work slaves the rest of our days.'

'But this Mantee — ' a man began. But Holt cut him off.

'Listen to me, you boneheads. If Hart is recruitin' help in the shape of this gunslinger, I say its odds on he'd also be recruitin' someplace else. The bastard figures we're gettin' too strong, and if there's truth in the Scavenger rumor, then he could go under unless he's got backin' to the hilt . . . '

He paused as a man with arms as thick as an average man's thighs raised a gnarled hand. 'What is it, Jack?'

'I gotta tell you that Hart's pretty woman claims she'd be just as pleased if this Mantee never shows on account she fears he can stir up twice as much trouble in a town as he might try and stop. Yet Hart, who's supposed to be straight, is behind him. What are we to make of this?'

Fort's brutish brow furrowed belligerently. For a long heavy minute the big man stood massaging his chin, his brow wrinkled like an old prune. Then he sharpened, staring at each man in turn and breathing loudly through flaring nostrils, like an old bull in a pen.

He suddenly brightened at a thought.

'By glory, boys, I'm suddenly thinkin' this whole thing could be a big pointer to the first chink in Hart's armour we've ever seen. How do I figger? Plain as daylight. If he feels he needs this sort of backin', then that means we finally got the stiff-necked son of a bitch bastard scared. Make sense to you?'

They said it did. Solid sense. And they were attentive and eager as big Fort took a seat, motioned them closer and dropped his tone to a confidential level. He'd reached the stage where he just wasn't willing to continue as they'd been doing much longer, he told them. Working twelve-hour shifts in death-trap mines and getting beaten up, kicked and humiliated at every turn by the boss's gun-stooge.

'It's time for me and time for all of us,' he summarized dramatically, thudding a ham fist on the rickety table, the light burnishing the leathery face. 'To decide if we're content to live like curs creepin' between Hart's long legs with our tails tucked in . . . or else like timberwolves that go for the throat, by God!'

As was always the case with meetings such as this, the evening quickly degenerated into a rip-roaring drinkup highlighted by arguments, fist-fights and the eventual arrival on the scene of the sheriff.

With Hart standing tall and solemn beneath the smoking oil-lamps, his long-fingered hands resting on gun handles as he ordered them out, not even Fort was about to challenge or resist.

Not right now, leastwise.

Yet the seeds had been sown. Having convinced first himself and then the others that their nemesis was manifesting the first serious signs of uncertainty and self doubt, Holte Fort would now be content to play the waiting game. He expected Hart to continue to strut and pose and maybe even crack the odd arm or skull in execution of his 'duty'. But he would be watched twenty-four hours a day, and the moment he revealed signs of the weakness in himself which Holte Fort now knew to be present, they would come down on him like a rock fall at the Copper King mine.

* * *

Mantee grunted, 'What do you make of him?'

'The kid?' Carson answered, tightening the horse's cinch strap. 'He's hard to read. Looks like nothing much, but then there's those bodies.'

154

'I smell owlhoot.'

'Maybe.'

'And gun-punk.'

Carson stroked his horse's silky muzzle. It was early morning at Overman mine and they were readying for their last leg to Sundown, watered, fed, rested and mounted at last. He was thoughtful as he gazed towards the doors.

'He could be more than just that,' he speculated. 'Seems to me he might be just putting on that awshucks country boy style as a cover. I've caught him watching us a couple of times, and he didn't look like a kid then. I guess I'll be just as pleased to see his back.'

Mantee finished with his saddling and leaned an elbow on his horse's hindquarters. 'Is he coming with us?'

'Don't think so. Guess he's worried about these men he shot and what Hart might make of it.' Carson's brows lifted. 'Did I say something funny?'

Mantee was almost smiling. 'He might be smart at that. Ethan's just the

155

kind of gunboy would-be that gets up
Jack's nose. I've seen him kick their
asses all over. I believe I'll advise him to
keep riding.'

They headed for the doors side by
side. The low-slanting rays of the rising
sun hit them in the eyes and they were
adjusting to the glare when they
suddenly became aware of the man. He
stood in the center of the weed-grown
quadrangle with the sun at his back, boots
apart, hat on the back of his head, hands
hanging loosely by his sides.

One swift glance passed between the
pair, for to men such as they this
studied pose was all too familiar. Ellis
Ethan looked ready to gunfight somebody. Yet how could this be?

'What?' Mantee growled with more
than a hint of warning in his tone.

The kid was grinning.

'One at a time or both together,
makes no nevermind to me. You can
take your time deciding . . . oldtimers.'

Carson and Mantee were stunned.
Yet the longer they stared, the more

clearly they realized that the kid with the long-barrelled shooter jutting from his shell-belt was serious. In the same instant they began moving apart, their faces rearranging into patterns of hard planes and angles as they confronted this challenge which seemed to have come out of nowhere.

'You loco?' Carson demanded.

'Better halt right there, gents,' Ethan said, his voice suddenly stronger, surer. 'That's fine. No, I ain't loco, Carson. Just doin' my job.' He couldn't suppress the grin. 'You see, I hold a contract on you, mister. From my people. My people heard somebody had hired you to come lend a hand in what's been happening in Sundown, so they did me the honor to send me and meet you half-way. You can just imagine my surprise when you fellers came out of the hell country and crossed my tracks by accident, and I found out who you were. It was like, y'know, fate.'

'You are looking to gunfight?' Mantee sneered.

'You're dead meat,' Ethan snapped back, meaner now, harder.

'I heard about you down at Sundown before your egg-suckin', whore-bred bastard lawman buddy got the jump and beat up on me. Hart seems to be relyin' on you — and so the miners are quakin' in their boots. Well, I owe Hart big time, dung-eater, and it's goin' to be sweet takin' you down first. And smart too, on account when I go back to square up with the sheriff I won't have to worry about his stinkin' best buddy mebbe sneakin' up behind me, will I?' His hands reached to his gunbutt and his pale face was a taut and deadly mask. 'I'm up to thirteen. You two'll tally me up to an even fifteen.'

'All right, all goddamn right!' Mantee snapped harshly. 'You want to die, we'll oblige. I hate your guts, punk, but even a nobody like you deserves to die fair. One at a time. Carson, you want first crack?'

'Yeah, Carson,' urged the kid. He had

hold of a live-wire edge and couldn't let go. 'First one for money, second for fun. Ready?'

Carson was angry but still didn't want this. He glanced at an impatient Mantee who spread big hands wide and began moving further off to one side, saying, 'By the book, punk. Any time you're ready is fine with me. One . . . '

Carson's face contorted as he realized it was going ahead whether he liked it or not. He hated Ethan now, not because he feared him so much as the fact that the kid was forcing him to kill him.

'Two!'

The combatants stood poised and ready in the sunlight waiting for the count of three which never came. Carson sensed rather than saw sudden movement off to his right in the shaved tip of a second before Mantee's .45 roared with fierce authority and Ellis Ethan's skull appeared to explode from within with blood, bone and gray matter erupting in a smoky spatter from above his right ear. With eyes bulging and his whole body seeming to collapse like something without bones, he crashed sideways, rolled over on to his face and was still.

'Another one you owe me,' Mantee smirked as he ejected the spent shell from his smoking gun.

'You bastard!'

The big man slipped his weapon into the leather and strolled across to look down at the dead man. 'Me? You must be joking, drifter. I did what had to be done.'

'That was murder.'

'Spare me the horsecrap. This weedy little prick blows in from nowhere and decides he wants to kill us, and you think we should take him seriously and treat him by the book? Beats me how you've stayed alive in your trade with buttermilk notions like that.'

'I might be a gunfighter but I'm not a hog butcher.'

Mantee got a toe under the corpse and rolled it over. He spat in the dead man's face, then arched a sardonic eyebrow at Carson. A sleeve was pulled up and both men saw the tattooed letter S on the pale forearm.

'Look at that,' Mantee triumphed. 'Scavenger! That's really why he came after us. You see, cleanskin? The ends always justify the means. He's dead and we're alive.'

'I could have killed him fair.'

'Ahh,' Mantee replied, making for the horses. 'There's the crux. What if you'd lost? Consider that. He'd be lining up on me now. And who's to know? Maybe he really was chain-lightning. Maybe if he'd killed you he could've killed me.' He swung up and tapped his forehead. 'I can see it's sinking in now. Coming?'

Slowly Shane Carson fitted boot to stirrup iron and heaved himself astride. The sun seemed to strike him like a hammer.

8

New Guns in Town

The sheriff walked to the far end of the street and halted. The smelters of Sundown burned yellow by day and red by night. The sun was high and dust was blowing across the Badlands the way it did most days this time of year. There was nothing to be seen to the west but heat, dust and distance, yet Hart remained there for some time as though he alone could see or hear something no one else could. Nothing the sheriff did went unnoticed in Sundown, and there were several citizens on hand, standing in the sparse shade of the blacksmith's shop, watching his tall figure through rippling heat waves. If ever one man had dominated here it was their badgeman.

'What do you figger he's lookin' fer

now?' speculated an old-timer from the shady porch of the Big Dipper. 'Trouble, mebbe?'

'What else is there?' grouched a bearded companion, a man mangled in the mines long ago who now spent his days smoking, and spitting and sipping on something for the pain. 'We got copper and we got trouble, and I'm a-thinkin' we ain't never gonna run shy of either.'

It was true that the veins of copper ran deep and seemingly endless directly beneath the town's red-dust streets. But whether the troubles which had first driven the town to import a town-tamer would last equally long was a matter of some debate.

Hart shaded his eyes.

The landscape beyond the town limits never varied. An arid panorama of severe erosion characterized by countless gullies, ridges and sparse vegetation baking under a searing sun, the eerie hues of the multicolored rock formations adopting changing shades and shadows as the sun marched across the sky. From where Hart planted bootheels deep in dust, the north trail curved gracefully away between twin stone bluffs, reappearing briefly about a mile further on as a slender yellow trace before vanishing altogether.

Nothing had come in from the north in over a week now. Thanks to the telegraph linking Sundown with Arrowhead, the sheriff knew that news of what had befallen the stage would have reached them up there by this time. The Bromfield Line had been proved reckless in dispatching a passenger coach at a time of high danger and was unlikely to make the same mistake again until someone signalled the all-clear.

He grunted. Most likely that decision would eventually have to come from him. He turned and retraced his steps back into town, a tall and sober man of forty dressed in gray, bronzed of feature and hard of eye. The wind seized upon the little puffs of dust raised by his boots and snatched them away to whatever limbo of the Badlands, where it deposited its eternal sweepings.

The sheriff of Sundown walked slower than he'd once done. His enemies claimed he was over the hill, and many a citizen believed he'd lost something vital over recent months.

Jack Hart believed that himself but was too proud and stiff-necked to admit it. But he had taken steps to improve his situation here, which if neither ethical or strictly legal, had worked for him in other hell-towns where he'd found the pressures and dangers mounting towards a point where they might overcome him. Wherever the sheriff signed on, he regarded the authority of the law as absolute. The irony was that he was sometimes prepared to break that very law in order to retain authority.

He saw the young woman emerge from the store to stand in the doorway looking his way. His lips tightened at the corners. Newcomer to town, she might well be pretty as a madonna and strong-willed as himself, yet he still wished she'd move on. Not that he didn't find Julia Lee attractive. He did. But her ongoing presence made him edgy for two reasons. For one, an unattached beauty here could only add to the tensions in a town where there were ten men to every female, and maybe one hundred to every woman not a whore.

The second reason was more personal. Miss Lee's simply being here as she awaited news on the fate of her fellow passengers from the stage was a constant reminder to the lawman of what might justly be construed as yet another failure on his part.

Since taking over here he'd characteristically come to regard the entire Badlands region of this county as his personal responsibility. This despite the fact that the terms of his appointment designated him specifically as sheriff of the town of Sundown and not one inch beyond. Yet the lawman believed, and had certainly proved in other places, that the peacemaking effects of having strong law in some town or another should ideally exert a beneficial effect across the whole region. You came down hard on the wild elements in a town, more often than not they shifted someplace else and suddenly the trails, ranches and mining-camps became as safe as the towns themselves.

In Hart towns, that was. For the sheriff hammered the law home hard, harder than most towns ever experienced. But not, or so it would seem only to his obsessive eye, perhaps not hard enough.

They met at the corner as Julia intended they should.

'No sign, Sheriff?'

He doffed his hat, the sun glinting from gray-flecked hair.

'Not yet, Miss Lee. Going my way?'

The town paused in its morning activities as six feet of somber peace officer and a young woman, who stood out here like a jewel in dust, went by.

Like any remote community, Sundown

thrived on gossip. But there was nothing to link the sheriff with the Buckhorn Hotel's young guest. The lawman was a one-woman man and Ava Pearl was herself a true beauty, although of a very different style from this young charmer.

At first the young studs from the Copper King mine and the Sister Fan had kept away from Julia in the belief that she was said to be here to meet up with her fiancé; and what prospects would rough miners with bad manners and dirty faces have with a woman like her anyway? But things had changed some since it became known that the wedding was cancelled. At least the bachelors now thought about asking her for a date even if none had quite worked up the nerve to actually do it.

Hart had no talent for small talk but the girl more than made up for that. She insisted on being brought up to date on anything he might have heard of activities in the Badlands since they spoke last, and he'd already learned that when this very feminine but determined young lady wanted something it was best to give it over or she could keep at you like a dog worrying a bone. 'I hear reports of marauders, gun battles, strange smokes from time to time . . . places burning . . . Injuns . . . sightings of badmen, drifters. That enough for you for one morning, miss?'

They halted before the jailhouse, a long, low building of an identical color to the street.

'I'm afraid I consider it very remiss of you not to organize a search party to look for Mr Carson and Mr Mantee, Marshal.'

She had been building up to this for some time but now it was out. He stared down at her with his thumbs hooked in his vest pockets, his gun handles glinting in the sun.

'Only a fool would go out there at this time, Miss Lee. Indeed, only a fool — or a ship of fools — would have set off from Arrowhead having been warned that the trails were unsafe.'

Julia's cheek-bones colored slightly.

'Strange that you can speak such a way about Mr Mantee, your close friend, Sheriff Hart.'

'Duke was loco to make that trip as well as you others. I said so at the time and I say so now.'

'I gathered from the way he spoke on our journey that he regards you as the finest friend a man could have, and that he was anxious to get to Sundown as he'd heard you were having difficulties here and might welcome a little moral support.'

It was rare that Hart was ever seen at a disadvantage. A slow flush of color appeared beneath his tan as he nodded, a sure sign of annoyance.

'My remarks still stand. If I left town to search for a friend and rioting erupted here, I'd be responsible.'

'It must be wonderful to be so cool and sensible at all times, Sheriff Hart. Cool, that is, apart from your occasional outbreaks of ferocity. I still would like to know what you intend doing about those missing men.'

'Not a thing. With regrets, of course.'

'Then I shall say good-day, Marshal.'

'Your servant, Miss Lee.'

From his window table at the Big Dipper, Tal Fawcett sat watching as Julia came back up the sloping street. He shook his lean head and fingered his mustache as he looked at Dick Grid seated opposite.

'She doesn't give up easy, does she?' he commented.

'Curious about her, don't you reckon?' replied the drummer. 'I mean, you and me was plenty upset about leavin' them fellers thataway, even though we had no choice. But we've accepted it. This is the Badlands, after all. Howcome she ain't accepting it?'

The other's eyes narrowed. 'What are you driving at?'

Grid spread calloused palms. 'A girl travels all this way only to find her fiancé has up and left on her, yet she checks in here in a hell-town and starts in frettin' over a pair of strangers who are likely long dead and gone . . . '

'So?'

The big man leaned back and took a pull on his beer. 'I say she fell for one or both of 'em. Only thing that makes sense.'

'Well, you sure don't, mister. Seems to me you're talking like a fool . . . Say, what is that woman doing now?'

Julia had suddenly lifted her skirts from the dust and begun to run. Immediately the two rose and hurried out on to the gallery to watch as she continued on down the center of the street, running westward and waving a gloved hand.

They raised their eyes and stiffened as they saw the two riders coming down the trail, ragged, sun-blackened, slump-shouldered and yet unmistakable.

'It's them!' Fawcett shouted, jumping into the street. He hauled his pistol and pumped a shot into the brassy sky. 'It's Carson and Mantee, by God! It's a miracle.'

Turning his head as citizens poured into the street, Dick Grid saw the sheriff back on the street, yet he barely recognized him. The at times forbidding town-tamer was not just grinning but laughing with relief, just like any lesser mortal might.

★　★　★

A chill had blown in off the Badlands when the sun went down but for once there was no dust, so that the air was clean and sweet now as Sheriff Hart and Duke Mantee strolled back from supper at the Frypan café.

As far as the eye could see beneath the bright full moon in any direction, the Badlands lay empty of all life as it sprawled into distance like some vast beast still panting from the heat of the day just past.

By contrast Broadway was crowded tonight, by those abroad to celebrate the survival of two men given up for lost, and also those hardcases who'd fervently hoped the lawman's alleged best friend and volunteer sidekick would never make it.

Men lounged in groups along the plankwalk in the central block, leaned up against saloon fronts or perched on the tie rails where the horses were tethered. Their voices were either animated or subdued, depending upon whether they were towners or miners.

Glowering miners fell silent as the tall sheriff and his even taller and larger companion passed by. For many it was their first glimpse of Mantee and they found the sight anything but reassuring. Bathed, shaved, barbered and sporting a new store-bought outfit of striped twill trousers and a fancy cotton shirt, Mantee, with his thick silver thatch and mahogany complexion, radiated the same kind of aura as the lawman only on a larger scale.

As the walkers passed through the thin stripes of light thrown out by the louvred doors of the Big Dipper, other groups paused to watch them go by, the buzz of conversation not breaking out again until the pair were out of earshot.

Some commented on Mantee's presence but most of the talk was focused on local events.

Rumor had it that five men had perished out at the Overman, a bunch of desert raiders and the kid the marshal had booted out of town, Ellis Ethan. Details were sketchy but it was also reported that the sheriff was satisfied with the survivors' account of the killings, and was prepared to allow the matter to rest at that.

Even wealthy copper kings and civic leaders rarely challenged Hart on anything, even though at times it appeared he enforced his law and order with a sledgehammer when a fly-swatter would do.

So a bunch of scalp-hunters and a hot-head gun kid were dead? So the world had to be a better place.

The Boar's Head saloon catered to Sundown's well-to-do, and when the two men walked in for a drink they were applauded. Everyone was by now aware of the association between Hart and Mantee, and many regarded the big man's survival and arrival as an omen pointed towards better times under an even stronger hand from the jailhouse. Sure, the sheriff was managing to keep the Cousin Jacks in check alone, but how much easier might it be for him with a fellow like this around, even simply for moral support?

'They like you, Duke,' Hart remarked as they raised their glasses in response to the toasts being offered in their direction. He smiled. 'Something of a novelty for you, eh?'

'And then some,' Mantee replied with a sardonic twist of the lips. 'But it won't last.'

He sounded sure. For the truth of it was, arrogant and overbearing Duke Mantee was a man with mighty few friends anyplace. For it was never enough for a man to be handsome, successful and strong, as he surely was; he must also be prepared to give and take, to curb his worst impulses and guard his wayward tongue in order to build bridges to others, skills and talents which Duke Mantee at times appeared to totally lack.

And unbeknown to the Boar's Head clientele, and possibly not even suspected by Hart himself, unpopularity and its consequences was the principle reason Mantee had sold up a thriving saloon in Tragg City, Wyoming and headed for Sundown.

By some weird accident or chemistry, Mantee and Hart had hit it off up north right from the get-go. And although he would fry in hell before he would admit it to a living soul, that was the principle reason that brought Mantee to this outpost of Hell.

He simply needed to see a friendly face.

The brandy was smooth and the conversation flowed easily. There were mutual acquaintances, old times, the Badlands adventure and the situation here in town to catch up on, debate, share opinions about.

Then suddenly Hart turned sober as Mantee set up another round.

'This has to be said, so I might as well say it quick, Duke. I've reined this place in and I've got the Jacks doing as I want, most times. I've hit hard, I'll allow, but I've only hit as hard as it takes. I appreciate your coming but I don't want you horning in. I don't need it, and as we found in other places, it can lead to complications. Understood?'

'Sure,' came the glib response. Mantee shrugged powerful shoulders and gave a wink as he emptied his glass at a gulp.

Hart meant what he said, he knew. But what he knew even more surely, was that circumstances could change cases. He'd given Sundown a good look-over, had sniffed the dust and scented out the danger and smouldering antagonism. He nodded sagely.

Sooner or later Jack Hart would need him and he would be there.

The batwings opened and both men turned in some surprise as Shane Carson entered with Julia Lee on his arm.

Although Hart anticipated Mantee's remarkable revival from their ordeal, he was astonished to see that Carson also appeared every bit as buoyant and vigorous in dark-blue shirt and new Levis. Or should he be surprised? he mused. Mantee and Carson were likely cut from pretty much the same cloth, even if they acted more like enemies than trail partners.

But the lawman only measured out so much friendliness when Julia dragged her escort across to the bar, with all eyes following. The fact that Carson appeared to be some kind of drifter with a gun arriving here unheralded and uninvited was sufficient reason for the sheriff to be wary of the man, suspicious even. Gunslingers came after the marshal from time to time when he trod on too many toes, and consequently he treated all the breed as potential enemies.

'We're dining in back, gentlemen,' Julia announced brightly. 'Would you care to join us?'

'Mantee's likely got something on, Julia,' insisted Carson, flashing his 'get lost' grin at the big man. 'Right?'

'Heck, this throws my plans right out,' Mantee joked to Julia. 'I intended asking you out tonight myself.' He was half-smiling but his eyes were cold as they flicked back to Carson. 'You know, maybe it's time I called in my markers with you, drifter . . . '

'What markers would they be, Duke?' Hart asked curiously.

'Well, I guess I just about lost count of the times I saved this roughnut's neck out there in the boondocks,' Mantee replied. 'Wouldn't you agree, gunman?'

Carson glanced sideways at the girl to gauge her reaction to the words. She appeared unfazed. Or maybe that was just wishful thinking on his part. He wasn't ashamed of his profession. Far from it.

But it could play hell with a man's friendships, especially the occasional high-class kind.

'Is this true, mister?' asked the bartender. 'Mr Mantee saved your life?'

'More times than I could count,' Carson said sardonically. Then he added enigmatically: 'Whether I needed it or not, in at least one case.' He glanced sideways at Hart. He was still sizing up the marshal of Sundown, and possibly vice versa. 'I guess you'd have to be relieved that Ethan the Scavenger kid won't be around to pose a threat any longer, Sheriff?'

'Of course.'

The peace officer appeared ready to say more, but Carson turned away sharply to the girl. Right now he'd had his fill of hard times and sudden death, didn't even want to discuss such matters.

He was alive.

The night was young.

He'd been astonished and delighted to find Julia still in town. She had broken up with her fiancé and had been waiting almost a week in Sundown for him and Mantee to show up. He was deeply impressed by that; he was also hungry as a horse. If all these factors didn't augur well for a memorable night then he doubted he would ever enjoy one. 'Ready, Julia?'

She smiled and made her good-nights to the two men who stood in silence watching them vanish through the frosted glass doors of the dining annex.

'Good style of girl,' Hart remarked, finishing his drink. 'And one mighty formidable gunman, I'd think.'

'He's a nothing,' Mantee snapped. 'Hey, you're not leaving are you, Jack? We have a lot of catching up to do.'

'We sure have. Unfortunately, as you saw on the street, the Jacks are chewing on mean meat tonight, as always. I've got to go show the flag to make sure they keep them in line. Take care and I'll see you tomorrow, man. Good to have you in town.'

A change came over Mantee as he remained at the long bar drinking with this one and that one who came up to congratulate him on their exploits in the Badlands. It was great to be in this dangerous town, Mantee reflected, but somehow less so than it could have been. Hart appeared pleased to see him, yet seemed intent on keeping their friendship and his job separate. The sight of Carson and Julia Lee together irritated him, for she was something special and he supposed he lusted after her ripe young body.

He brooded. In the Badlands, things had happened so fast, and simple survival had proved such a challenge, that there had been no time for him to lapse into one of his dark moods for which he was notorious. Now there was time to unwind and think things over, he could feel the familiar shadows drawing in, recognized the old hints and warnings.

He seemed to withdraw from the glad-handers and his surroundings, to feel again the burden of self-knowledge and that inward-turning stare that depressed him. Once again he was staring along a corridor that ran far back into a sinister room filled with secrets and the sulphurous stink of his own shortcomings and secret guilts.

Suddenly he flung from the room with such force that drinkers went to the windows to watch as he halted on the porch glaring at a group of miners. The miners stared back and Mantee took exception.

'I'm told you maggot-eaters are hatching up something,' he accused, approaching threateningly. 'That you have a gripe against the sheriff and that just maybe you might be looking to harm him in some way. Would that be right, maggot-eaters?'

These were hard men and yet they backed away. Mantee was too big. He was too aggressive and sure of himself. And rumor had it that he had apparently put too many men under the ground in other places and was too closely allied with the marshal. Only one man, a comparative newcomer, saw fit to stand his ground and take exception, a young miner with muscular arms and the punched-in face of a fighter.

'You can't talk to us like that, peckerhead!'

Foolish man.

Mantee's Colt jumped into his fist and slashed him across the face. As the miner reeled sideways, Mantee delivered a brutal kick to the belly, doubling him over in agony, one arm flailing. The barrel rose and fell again and everyone heard the arm break as it made contact. The man screamed and passed out as the Colt, now cocked, swung wide to cover the shocked miners.

Mantee grinned whitely at them.

'Come on,' he begged, but they didn't move. The gun spun in a whirling arc on his trigger finger and was driven back into the holster. Mantee spread his empty hands. 'Now?' he taunted, but there were still no takers.

Slowly the big figure straightened. He kicked the motionless figure at his feet. Everyone was staring at him now. When he swung to meet the eyes that watched from the windows and doors of the saloon, the faces were no longer friendly or admiring, and he saw that his brief moment of acceptance had already quickly passed.

9

The Sheriff's Friend

The Copper King mine-boss, Coster Daley, sniffed at the sudden stink and stared up from his desk at the visitor his bodyguards ushered into his inner office. The blinds were drawn and nobody from the mine had seen this grisly stranger come, nor would they see him leave. Even a man of Daley's wealth, power and status would invoke the full wrath of the law were it to be known he was on speaking terms with the clan boss of the Scavengers.

'You ready or not, Mawby?'

Daley never wasted words. He was a sawed-off toad of a man with eyes like steel buttons and a brusque manner.

By contrast, the tall man standing before him looked more wolf than man, lank-haired, with sunken cheeks and lantern jaw. Mawby had lived like a wild animal in the deserts and mountains most of his life, and looked it.

'Bin ready fer a week,' came the guttural reply. 'You ready fer us or ain'tcha?' Daley looked away, suddenly slumping. He was a desperate man tonight. He'd driven the miners to the point of rebellion and there was every sign that one more incident or fatality might precipitate the mass riot that had been threatening for months.

If it erupted, the law might not be able to halt it. Which was the reason why the rich man was now doing business with a man unfit to be fed to the mine dogs. 'How many men can you muster' he demanded.

'Close to forty.'

Daley got to his feet. 'Keep them on stand-by.'

'Where's me money?'

'We agreed you'd be paid after if I have to call on you.'

A filthy hand extended. 'I've changed the agreement. One thousand now and another if we git to go into action.'

Daley swung on a flunkey. 'Give him his money and kick his scraggy arse out of here. Then send someone in with the disinfectant.'

'Always a pleasure to do business with a regular gent,' the Scavenger croaked, and was tonguing the sheaf of bills like a bull licking a salt block as they bundled him out.

⋆ ⋆ ⋆

Ava of Ava's Fashions on Broadway was beautiful, as everyone agreed. She ran a successful business, could handle drunken miners as if they were schoolboys, and loved the sheriff of Sundown.

But love or even simple affection appeared to be in short supply when she strode into the law office that evening about supper-time, and dismissed two young deputies with an imperious jerk of her head.

'Don't start,' the man at the desk warned.

'Why?' she demanded, hands on hips and dark eyes shining hard. 'Come on, come on, I just want the simple truth. Why?'

Nobody spoke to Jack Hart that way. Customarily, that was. But when Ava was angry, as she plainly was tonight, she would talk exactly how she pleased to anybody.

'It's not what you think, honey,' the sheriff said, rising. 'Duke just came down to visit.'

'The way he did at Bonanza?'

'Things got out of hand there, I'll allow. But — '

'Did you invite him here?'

'Er, no, 'course not.'

'You hesitated!' she accused, then suddenly seemed to lose momentum. She sat on the arm of a ragged leather chair and stared up at him, shaking her head. 'I could see it all coming, Jack. The job was getting too much for you but you were too stubborn and proud to admit it . . . to even ask for help. Damn your vanity! So you allow

Mantee to come here, knowing what it must lead to, knowing . . . '

Her voice broke and a tear showed in her magnificent eyes. The sheriff of Sundown stood before her, looking as the town never saw him, uncertain, apologetic.

'Honey, it doesn't have to be as bad as you're painting it. OK, I'll admit Duke could help intimidate these miners, and that could help me keep them in line. But there doesn't have to be any gunplay — '

'There's always gunplay wherever he goes.'

'But — '

'Don't 'but' me, Jack. Just hold me and tell this won't end up like Bonanza, even though we both know it must.'

The sheriff said what she wanted to hear and stood stroking her hair and staring at the window. By the harsh light of the hanging brass lamp he looked almost like an old man.

★ ★ ★

It was still well before cock-crow as Shane Carson made his solitary way along the hushed, false-fronted canyon that was Broadway.

Nothing stirred, the very stillness almost discordant to an ear and eye desensitized by the unrolling violence of the Badlands; he was taking time to readjust to the muted feverishness and erratic pulsebeat of this ugly town. His ear detected no hoofbeat, coyote cry, the tinkle of breaking glass or the whimpering cry someplace, which could be all the warning a man might receive before something unstoppable should erupt behind weather-warped walls then burst out into the street with a roar like floodgates giving way.

If Sundown was half as bad as he'd been led to believe by his superiors, that was.

Perhaps it had been this unnatural quiet that had awakened him in the small hours of his third night in town. Then again it might have been something as simple as the fact that he'd finally caught up with his sleep after the rigours of the Badlands.

Or something even more sinister maybe? whispered the back of his mind. Perhaps something like his highly developed instinct for danger was kicking in again? He paused beneath one of six flickering Rager lamps to consider that latter possibility.

He was rested, he reflected calmly. Sundown had lapsed into a kind of uneasy armistice with itself, while Shane Carson, the covert trouble-shooter, was once again beginning to feel energy starting to surge.

So how come he wasn't relaxed?

He suspected now that it had been an underlying nagging restlessness or even suspicion that had caused him to jerk upright in his hotel bed at three in the morning, fully awake and keyed up with his brain fully engaged and searching for answers. But he was still no closer to identifying a single root cause for his unrest as he moved on past Applegate's Mercantile, the post office, then on towards the shadowed bulk of the stage depot shouldering high against a lowering sky.

Nothing to stop him throwing a leg across a good horse and heading off, or was there?

Thunder growled in the north and a solitary hound-dog appeared from beneath the elevated boardwalk before the Buckhorn Hotel to stare, ready to run when the man stopped to gaze up at the darkened windows, where Julia slept beneath the same roof as Ava Pearl, Mantee, and several additional hardmen imported to help keep the peace at the Copper King mine. Heading down to Sundown following the shoot-out at the Overman in company with Mantee, a badly burnt-out Shane Carson had envisioned himself attacking a huge meal, then maybe grabbing twenty four hours' quality sleep, which just might set him up for whatever was awaiting him at the town at the dead end of the line. Twenty-four hours' bunk-time away from the Badlands, where he'd seen more trouble than on a dozen jobs. Away also from the tetchy sheriff, from the obvious misery and injustices being suffered by the miners, from the strange feeling of something hanging, brooding, over the town. And, and most of all, away from Mantee.

Not only that, he'd wired Rosalee County instructing his superiors to select another man to help them sort out their troubles here, on account of the fact that he was virtually burnt out before arrival.

His occupation as listed on the books of the undercover governmental bureau in Rosalee County appeared bland enough on paper: Mediator.

This suggested a gentleman, possibly scholarly, who might visit a trouble-spot, light up his pipe and proceed to move about calmly, assessing rights and wrongs before bringing the fractious parties together and hammering out a neat solution to their problems.

The reality of what was expected of

Shane Carson on assignment could scarcely have been more different. The bureau sent him into places where more often than not the only effective mediation required proved to be that achieved by harsh words, a fist in the face or a storm of gunshots.

Still of a mind to quit if and when his replacement should arrive, he kept insisting to himself that he could not care less about the sheriff's uneasy grip on control, the miners' militant tribalism, feeding on a festering sense of injustice, the implacability of the mine-owners and, just to add the clincher, rumors of increased Scavenger sightings in the region.

This town was like a powder-keg ready to blow. So why didn't he simply get hold of a good horse and head off, with or without permission or replacement?

He knew only too damn well.

One, he was no quitter. Two, she was still here. He told himself that until he understood exactly why Julia Lee seemed to hold him as though by an invisible chain, this dust-stricken wide place in the trail would not let him go. Such thinking was unfamiliar territory for the man of the gun whose restless energies and the demands of his profession always kept him on the move.

What was he really thinking?

That Julia might have chosen to stay on here after her man did a runner because she was interested in him, Shane Carson?

He scowled. Sure, he'd made a big play for her and they'd stepped out together a couple of times since his arrival, and it had been good, even real good. But just shuffling a deck of cards didn't constitute a poker-game any more than shining up to a pretty woman constituted a romance, he advised himself soberly. He wondered if Bat Masterson had gotten it right when he'd said, 'When a Colt .45 is the first thing you love it turns out to be the only thing.'

He moved on faster as though trying to outstrip his thoughts, realized belatedly that the eastern sky had begun to lighten. The day's first lamplights now showed inside the Gunsight saloon, in the flophouse opposite, and down at the plank-and-batten hospital.

The city water-wagon appeared in the ghostly gray light with the driver hunched miserably on his plank seat scratching at his bushy gray beard with the whip handle. When the vehicle passed it left behind an eight-foot-wide strip of the street darkened by the spray. But the dust of Sundown was eternal. It would rise again, as it did every day, to climb the hot sky and haze the sun before once again descending in the evening cool to settle gently over rooftops, back alleys, workshops, smithies, barns and corral.

He stopped again to study the single fresh bullet hole in the barber shop's front wall inches below the window. Day before yesterday a miner with a skinful threatened a citizen with a rusty old gun. He was swiftly and expertly disarmed by the sheriff but not before the Jack touched off this one wild shot.

This random-seeming incident had resulted in a bunch of drunken miners attempting to whip up a protest march. They might have succeeded but for Mantee. Carson had seen the man appear from nowhere in a fine new broadcloth jacket and vest, to smash the leader's jaw with just one punch. He'd then stepped back with one hand on his gun handle, which was all it took to disperse the mob, even though Carson's sharp eye had detected the genuine rage and hatred coming off the troublemakers like heat from a cookstove.

When the sheriff had shown on the scene in time to see the injured man picked up and carted off to hospital, he'd appeared impressed by Mantee's intervention. But of course he'd have to be. They were boon companions and veterans of other such wild towns, so how could he not now be pleased to boast a Right Bower he could rely upon in this deadly game in which he, of course, must always be deemed to be in the right?

A curious situation, he reflected now.

Mantee had already bought up a saloon on West Street and identified himself as a saloonkeeper. The town seemed to accept this at first but it didn't take long to realize that the flashy hard man saw himself first and foremost as the sheriff's shadow.

But if this was the case, why didn't Hart openly admit Mantee was here at his behest to help him through a particularly troublesome time?

Already, Carson believed he knew the answer.

Hart had a reputation which was plainly warranted. To solicit help overtly could tarnish that reputation critically upon the streets. But simply to have a friend to back your play now and again was a totally different matter.

But was it smart?

Carson, the professional, had already

formed the opinion that Jack Hart was too old for this job and that the situation he was attempting to control could be close to getting out of hand.

If he was right about that, then did he, Shane Carson, really have any right to seek to be replaced?

'Why don't you just get on with what they expect of you here, Carson?' he demanded. And answered himself, 'Yeah, why not?'

He almost grinned, aware that he already felt better for a good, self-administered sharp talking-to.

Suddenly he stiffened and cocked his head at the sound of distant wheels. His first thought was that it must be the water-cart returning, but it eventually proved to be a dray rumbling in from the Copper King carrying one dead and three injured following yet another cave-in.

Walking behind the vehicle in almost military array, a squad of miners led by battered Holte Fort trudged slowly in grim-faced ranks, grimed faces bathed in the first rosy glow of day which now hazed the eastern sky.

The men marched in time and didn't speak. Carson's trained ear seemed to detect the underlying pulse of Sundown lift and change until eventually, in his imagination, it seemed to be tolling as loudly and ominously as the great iron bells of the Cathedral of the Saints in Taos at a requiem mass. As the procession passed he grew aware that all along the street people were drifting out on to porches, galleries and boardwalks to stand and stare.

He felt his neck hair lift slightly at the sight.

Had the town also caught the sulphur stench of upheaval and rebellion in the very air, or were they just simply curious? And — even more important — did Shane Carson really give a damn one way or another?

He knew the answer. Suddenly the last of his weariness was completely gone. His duty lay clear before him and he felt as ready for the challenge as he'd ever been. His eye was clear, his jaw set hard as he turned his head to watch the brass ball of the sun appear far out across the dun-colored plains to begin its stately march across a day that would prove unlike anything Sundown had ever seen before.

★ ★ ★

'What happened?' Carson demanded.

'There was another fall-in, of course,' slurred the miner awaiting treatment at the hospital. 'That number three shaft is a goddamn grave — '

'What happened afterwards?' Carson cut in. By now the news that there had been yet another disaster out at the Copper King had spread and the whole town was in uproar about it. But Carson had just learned of the trouble immediately following the incident, which sounded more serious than the rockslide itself. 'There was a riot?'

'Somethin' like that. Fort got the men all worked up and then someone started on the administration block with an axe. The security guards, well . . . ' The man looked away. 'They shoulda had better sense than to horn in the way they did. They could see the mood, how sore everyone was . . . '

'So you killed them?'

'One dead and the other stove up. But honest to God we were calmin' down when Hart and that damn flash pard of his showed, that bastard Mantee!'

Carson's face was taut as he watched the injured shuffling in and out, occasionally catching glimpses of Julia and Ava amongst other women assisting in the emergency. But he was listening carefully, hearing for the first time exactly what had taken place as opposed to all the hysterical accusation and counter accusation that had the town seething.

It now seemed plain it had been the sight of Mantee with the sheriff that had touched the lucifer to the tinder for the miners. Hart was the law, harsh and uncompromising though he might be, but to the diggers and indeed to most of Sundown by this, Duke Mantee was viewed with dismay as some kind of loose cannon without status and with respect for nobody but the marshal, who allowed him to act like some kind of unpaid and unsworn deputy.

'The sheriff came in hard like he always does, Carson. You know, crackin' heads and warnin' us all to get our asses back to town fast while he straightened things out out there. We were doin' what he said, too, but a couple of the boys wasn't quick enough to suit Mantee. He put the boot into a driller, the feller rounded on him and stopped a slug in the shin for his trouble. Suddenly everyone was ragin' again and one of the boys let fly at Hart with a hammer that knocked his hat off . . . '

His voice faded away. Carson stared at him, sensing what was coming next. 'And?'

'Mantee rode the man down then

shot him twice through the heart, so he did. It was murder, Carson. Nobody'll ever be able to call it anythin' else.'

Carson was not about to defend Duke Mantee. Not after the killing of Ellis Ethan, he wasn't.

He asked grimly: 'What did the sheriff do?'

'Do? Why, he looked sore, that's what he done. Might have even looked shocked. Spoke real sharp to Mantee, so he did, and the big feller didn't like it one little bit. But when we left to bring the hurt men in, them two was stridin' around together out there givin' orders and pushin' people about just like nothin' had happened.'

The miner paused, his eyes intense on his face.

'You was lost in the Badlands with this bastard, Carson. Just exactly what breed of skunk is he? And howcome a man like that lawman and him are such pals? I've seen Hart dunk better men than Mantee in the trough and boot their asses all the way up Broadway when he wants to make a point. None of us can figger this. Can you?'

Carson shook his head. No.

He turned sharply as a man with a strapped-up leg and leaning on a crutch emerged in the company of two curly-headed and wild-eyed miners, one of whom had a .45 thrusting up from the waistband of his moleskins. They nodded to him respectfully, for he had been established as something of a hero following the Badlands saga, a fact that mildly amused Carson yet seemed to infuriate Mantee.

'We're meetin' at the Boar's Head, Eli,' the one with the gun said to the miner. 'All of us, and now!'

They left. It seemed that at long last the patching, repairing, splinting, medicating and bandaging on a vast scale was almost done.

'Gotta go, Carson.'

Shane seized the fellow's sinewy arm. 'Tell them I said not to start anything they can't finish.'

'There's a hell of a lot of us, mister.

And we've had enough. We been complainin' about the safety for a year and men keep dyin' in the shafts 'most every week. We kept protestin' and marchin', so the copper-bosses and the money men bring in a killer with a badge. Then men keep gettin' hurt, and when we get angry Hart kicks the crap out of us. Now we have another real bad accident and instead of somethin' to help us, a whiff of understandin' mebbe, what do we get? Good men beat up and one murdered in cold blood afore our very eyes. And you say we oughtn't start nothin'? Makes a man wonder whose side you're on, and that's just too bad on account some of the lads figured you might be different somehow.'

A brooding Carson watched him go.

They were like children, he thought, great, brawny, tousle-headed children who bawled when hurt, responded if you treated them well, threw tantrums when things didn't go their way. Only thing, these childlike Herculeses were dying in this place, and he could envision even more bloodshed ahead should they be foolish enough to revolt against what was plainly gross mistreatment. When Julia emerged eventually she found him sipping on a bottle of beer as he surveyed the street. She had been working four hours straight, yet somehow managed to appear as fresh, cool and tempting as a mint julep. He liked the way she acted just as though she expected to find him waiting, was taken by surprise when she rose on tiptoes to kiss his cheek.

'What's that for?' he asked.

'I'm not sure.' She smiled, linking her arm through his as they started off. 'I suppose, truth to tell, there's so much about you I'm not sure of, isn't there?' He halted to stare down at her face and for a moment all of it — the knots of sober-faced men, the passing horsemen and the oppression hanging over the town like a storm-cloud — were suddenly as if they no longer existed.

This was plainly reality time for

Shane Carson. Time for questions and answers and getting things straight before ... before what? Before Sundown spontaneously erupted like old explosives left out too long sweating in the sun, maybe.

'Julia, why did you wait here instead of going on south?'

'Simple. You and Duke risked your lives to save us ... it was the least I could do.'

'No other reason?'

'What do you want me to say, Shane?'

'You broke off with your fiancé. We've been back three days, yet you are still here.'

'Is this leading up to something?'

'Let's leave while the going's good. How is that for something?'

'What if I said yes?'

'We'd go.'

'No we wouldn't.' Again she took his arm and they started off. She was looking directly ahead as she continued deliberately: 'You wired those people in

Rosalee County that you were prepared to continue on here after all, didn't you?'

He was startled. 'How did you know that?'

'Ava. The sheriff tells her things and she tells me. In confidence, of course. Hart's been checking up on you, Cash.'

His jaw thrust out. 'What the hell — '

'No, don't be annoyed. It seems everything he's been able to discover about you is good, which comes as no surprise to me.' She squeezed his arm. 'Remember when you described yourself as a peacemaker? Well, the records at the newspaper say that this is quite accurate. That you only carry a gun to help people who need it, much like the marshal when you come to think of it. And that is why you're still in Sundown, why you wouldn't leave with me even if I asked you. You're concerned about what's happening here, more worried than you'll tell me, and I believe you'll remain here until things have quietened down.' Now she looked at him. 'How close am I to the truth?'

'You make me sound nearly noble,' he said self-deprecatingly. 'A lot of people would disagree with you on that.'

'I believe in fighting for what is right,' she said, more serious than he had ever seen her. 'So many people know there's so much wrong in the West, but most only wring their hands and complain while things get worse. But if people fight for those things they should have then they have my admiration, no matter what means they are forced to use.'

Again they halted; this time it was he who stopped. A ruckus between miners and townsfolk had just broken off across the street, and someone was bawling for the law. Yet he was barely aware of the situation.

For this was a telling moment for him to realize that this woman seemed to understand what drove him when so many were prepared to dismiss him as just another gunfighter. He genuinely cared about the law and about people. But he was also a man of the gun, which made him a product of his time. She was the first woman of quality in a long time to regard him with anything but disgust. So he promptly took her in his arms and kissed her right then and there, and she surprised him for a second as she flung her arms round him and held him close, real close.

It seemed to last a long time and might have lasted even longer had not Carson sensed something, a change in tempo on the street, a sudden hush.

He broke away and glanced upwards to see the big figure on the high porch, sleekly handsome, big hands grasping the railing. The man wore a soft white shirt with full sleeves that must have set him back twenty bucks. His silver hair was perfect and the oiled bronze of his face glinted with reflections bouncing up off his shirt front.

He was staring down at Carson with eyes like drills.

'What?' Carson demanded, lowering his hands. He didn't trust this man now. Who could?

'Hello, Julia,' Mantee responded. 'Would you mind excusing me and this piece of dirt a moment?'

'Yes I would,' she cried. 'What on earth is wrong with you, Duke?'

'Wrong? I suppose what's wrong is seeing this bum hanging around you and you seeming to enjoy it. I thought you had more taste, refinement. I know he doesn't have enough class to feed hogs, but . . .'

At that moment the noisy wrangling continuing nearby erupted into violence, with a miner knocking a fat citizen off his feet then driving in with a kick. Mantee vaulted the railing like an athlete and hit the ground running, gun in hand. Without hesitation he charged headlong into the mob, cutting left and right with the barrel of the gun none had seen him draw. He had three men down and was pistol-whipping another when a shot rang out, bringing him whirling around, ready to fight.

It was Hart.

'Enough of that, Duke!' The lawman stood in the arcade entrance reloading his smoking gun. 'This is my duty and I'll take care of it.'

'But, Jack, I was just — '

'Just acting like a blamed fool, that's what you were doing, man,' the sheriff cut in. He jerked his chin. 'Get off the street and cool down. That's an order.' It was almost painful to watch Mantee's face as he held his ground disbelievingly for almost too long before suddenly whirling and lunging away. People jumped from his path. A miner shouted a jibe but Mantee didn't even look to see who it was. Carson had seen this man in savage mode before, but nothing like this.

*　*　*

The miners stood in brooding groups upon the basement stairs of the disused supply store on Catt Street, watching

Holte Fort as he slowly circled the broken table which supported a bottle with a candle thrust into its neck. Several miners wore guns but most were armed only with pick-handles or chunks of timber ripped from the crumbling walls.

'We got three options,' he stated grimly, his voice a flat monotone, holding down the emotion as all could see. 'First, we can go after the mayor and the mine boss and — '

His voice was drowned by a sudden roar of approval. He raised his hands for quiet, and got it. 'Second, we can roll up our gear and quit this town before we're all buried or maimed out there.' He waited for the reaction to this to fade, then rammed a finger into the air. 'Or third, and best, we can take one last stab at negotiatin'.'

This went down like a lead canoe. Negotiation had never been an option with the Copper King management; you either did it their way or you quit. Nobody knew this brick wall better than Fort, the man who'd gone cap in hand to Coster Daley on their behalf more often than he could remember. Their fury had been brought to white heat by Mantee's attack on Broadway, coming as it did hard upon the heels of the accident.

The Cousin Jacks wanted to rip and tear but Holte Fort had been down that dead-end street too often. Yet the man seemed confident as he calmed them down again, why, they couldn't guess. Once again men had been killed and mangled in the pits; once again the law had sided with those responsible. Their situation was seen as having deteriorated since the arrival of Duke Mantee, who aligned himself with Hart, presenting a gun force of two which only a truly desperate miner would dare challenge now, yet these were indeed truly desperate men. What they did not know was that Fort had a possible solution, which he revealed after lighting up a long thin cheroot. 'It's Carson, boys,' he announced with a suddenly expansive gesture. 'The hardcase gunman. Howcome we didn't think of him before this?'

They stared at him uncomprehendingly. Where did Carson figure in all this?

'The notion come to me when I first realized them two, Carson and Mantee, ain't buddies at all but hate one another's guts somethin' fierce. Then I got curious when Carson changed his mind about movin' on, and next thing I see him walkin' that Lee gal about — and it ain't no secret Mantee's got his eye on that filly too. But it wasn't until tonight when I happened to hear that Carson and Mantee was wranglin' over that skirt, that the film suddenly came off my eyes. Carson's surely some breed of gunfighter, or a gun for hire. It's plain he's for us, or leastwise he ain't tryin' to wipe us out, like Mantee is. We got a few bucks in the fund, and — jeeze, if we could just hire a geezer like him we might start gettin' some respect. Folks might take us serious at last and mebbe then Daley would just have to set down and listen. What do you say, boys?' The boys were thinking hard.

★　★　★

The young women often met at the eating-house off Broadway, Dottie's Squat and Gobble. Despite the name, Dottie's was a nice little retreat, much too fussy and feminine to attract miners or cowboys but perfect when women craved good coffee and a quiet place to chat.

Today there seemed to be one dominant topic of conversation, whether it be at Dottie's, the Big Dipper, the general store or anyplace else where people gathered. The latest violence at the mine was that topic. But having just spent several hours at the hospital attending the victims of that accident as well as the subsequent brawls in town, Julia and Ava avoided that subject, at least for a while, as they mulled over subjects far more interesting to young and attractive women the world over, namely their menfolk.

Jack Hart had been Ava's man for more than a year, while Julia had only begun to regard Shane Carson seriously following that main street kiss just an hour earlier.

Sundown might well be teetering on the edge of crisis but Julia couldn't help but look radiant as she apprised her friend of this latest exciting development in her life.

'I can't tell him yet, Ava, but I believe I fell in love with Shane the moment he boarded the stage that day. Or perhaps it was a little later when I realized just how fine and decent he was . . . '

'For a gunfighter, you mean?' Ava teased gently.

'For a man who believes in putting his life on the line for what he believes in, Ava,' Julia replied seriously. 'Just like Jack.'

'Jack,' Ava said reflectively, staring out the window. 'I just wish . . . '

'Wish what, honey? That Duke Mantee had never come here, perhaps?'

Their eyes met. Ava nodded.

'You're very perceptive, honey. Of course you're right.' She sighed and raised her cup. 'I don't like to criticize Jack, but I do wish he would retire. Nor do I like attacking Duke, because the man thinks so highly of Jack. And the fact that he saved his life once only makes it sound more unkind of me to wish him further away. But the point is that while Duke seems to need Jack, and thinks he is doing so much for him whenever he shows up at towns where he's working, I know Jack doesn't really need him. A tougher deputy, perhaps. But not Duke. He's . . . well I think you know now what he's like?'

Julia nodded her dark head. She knew Duke Mantee was attracted to her; she found him intensely interesting and very handsome in return, but that was as far as it went or could ever go. For surely that big brooding man was too turbulently unpredictable to be anything but of grave concern. And still, as ever, she found herself mystified by the Mantee-Hart connection. If the sheriff didn't want the partnership, why didn't he end it?

She put the question to Ava, who answered as best she felt she could.

'Duke is a strangely driven man, as we all know, and as he showed just an hour ago. He's arrogant and successful and he can be a big hit with the ladies, and most men with any brains are terrified of him. You would think a man with that sort of ego and abilities would want for nothing. But, you know, Julia, I have always sensed something almost pathetic beneath all that glitter and macho swagger.'

'Pathetic? Duke Mantee?'

'I know it must sound crazy. Yet I feel it every time I see him. And I think this is why he needs Jack's friendship. Jack, as we both know, is about the most highly regarded man in his line of work in the Territory. Or was, leastwise. Jack has friends all over the West but I sense

Duke has just the one — a man he can look up to and respect. Without Jack, I suspect Duke Mantee could wake up alone one morning and start in believing all the ugly but often truthful things people say about him, and decide it all wasn't worth the candle and, well, just throw the game in.'

'Are you serious, Ava?'

'Never more so in my life.'

It was at that moment that a cart overladen with drunken miners went rattling by, to go charging into Broadway, scattering pedestrians. The rig was brought to a halt and yet another fight erupted. Violence was breaking out constantly on a day where many storekeepers had closed down and boarded up their doors as the aftershock of the Copper King incident continued to resonate through the streets like trickles of fire threatening at any moment to erupt into a full conflagration.

Diners gathered at the windows to watch as swinging staves and fists saw figures bowled over, then jump up again and return to the fray.

The two tall men appeared in the blinking of an eye and Ava and Julia saw sunlight glint on gunbarrels as the marshal and Mantee accomplished exactly what Jack Hart was paid to do, namely, restore law and order. In mere moments it seemed the street was littered with hurt and unconscious figures, with two tall men standing over them.

'It would seem they've patched up their differences,' Julia remarked drily as the corner began to clear, allowing the traffic through again.

'They always do,' Ava replied, fingering her thick, blonde hair back from her face. 'Duke wouldn't have it any other way.'

'You make it sound almost as though the marshal couldn't get rid of Mantee even if he wanted to, Ava.'

'Didn't you do anything to get rid of him, Julia?'

'I . . . I do believe I have discouraged

Duke's attentions. I can't be certain.

'You see, talking to Duke as I do, I got to feeling he has a vision in his mind for himself and for this town. In this vision there are four people, two couples. Jack and me and you and him. His face lights up whenever he talks about it.'

'But that is so foolish!'

'I know. But who is going to convince Duke Mantee of that?'

★ ★ ★

A shadow fell through the diner doorway and Carson looked up to see Holte Fort standing there, staring at him. There had been no meeting planned between the two men but somehow Carson knew he had been expecting to see the miner tonight. He beckoned the haggard man across and ordered another two mugs of coffee.

10

Blood and Pride

'Come on, come on,' Mantee snarled at the bloody-nosed miner. 'Pay your crummy fine and get out. You're stinking up the place.'

The man did as ordered, as did the next in line. The third and last man arrested following the brawl on Broadway a short time earlier was ready to pay, but not in silence.

'This ain't right and you know it, Sheriff,' he told the lawman who was seated behind his desk. 'It was hard enough for us to accept you as genuine law when you first came, but at least you was hired by the council. But havin' a dude just come in off the desert and start beltin' us about and crackin' bones everyplace we show, that just ain't right.'

'How's this for right, dog's ass?' Mantee chimed in, taking the miner by the scruff and boosting him out the jailhouse door by the seat of his pants, where he disappeared with a clatter. Mantee brushed his hands together and turned to wink. 'If you let them gripe and grouch today, they are just as likely to come after you with a gun tomorrow, I always say, Jack. Unless they know who's boss, that is. Time for a jolt at the bar?'

The sheriff continued making entries in the jailhouse ledger in his neat strong hand.

'Another time, Duke.'

'But — '

'I've a lot to do.'

Mantee made to reply but bit his lip, grabbed down his hat and strode out the door. He paused to call back: 'I'll keep a sharp eye on things,' and was gone, bootheels thudding away to silence on the walk.

Hart leaned back in his chair and put finger and thumbs to the corners of his eyes. In unguarded moments like this the town-tamer looked much less like a man of legend than an everyday working man battling with the pressures of a tough job.

Yet in reality, the battle was already over, and Sheriff Hart felt he'd lost. Today, there was no longer any doubt in his mind. He had 'stayed too long at the fair'. The challenges were much the same as they had always been but he was no longer the man capable of meeting them head-on and turning things around.

He should quit, he told himself. But what would that achieve? Chaos, madness, maybe total destruction.

Inside he knew he was washed up. But who could run this hell-town?

Steps sounded on the porch and he was instantly composed again, sitting ramrod straight, features strong and reassuring when he turned his attention to his ledger as knuckles rapped the doorframe.

He looked up and said: 'Mr Carson.'

'Sheriff.' Carson entered and Hart gestured at a chair. Shane sat, removed his hat and rested it across his knees. 'Bad business.'

'Indeed.' Hart set the pen aside and rested his palms upon the cool blotter. 'What is it? And before you speak you might as well know the answer will probably be no.'

'You don't even know why I'm here yet.'

Hart reached into a drawer and withdrew a sheaf of notes clipped together. He tossed them on to the desk before him.

'Your past record, Mr Carson, or at least as much as I've been able to assemble.' He eyed Carson almost accusingly. 'You are a do-gooder, gunman. A champion of causes who envisions himself as a righter of wrongs and defender of the underdog, whereas in reality you're obviously just another hardcase hiring his gun. From the moment you showed in town I've been expecting a visit from you, and here you are, right on schedule. So, now we have that out of the way, why don't you tell me how much the Cousin Jacks are paying you to go against me?'

This was a bad start and it didn't get any better. Carson had no connection with the mine. He was here on official duty to try and prevent Sundown sliding into chaos. He would not reveal his official status. The field operatives of Headquarters swore an oath to work incognito.

Quietly and calmly he went ahead to suggest a meeting between Forte Holt, Coster Daley the mine owner, the sheriff and himself before it was too late. And no Mantee. He pulled no punches; it was too late to worry about treading on people's corns. He stared the grim badgeman in the eye and told him the worsening Sundown troubles now seemed to stem less from conflict between miners and management than from the exacerbating presence of Mantee.

He sat and awaited Hart's reaction.

After some moments the man rose to full height and tugged down his waistcoat, as stern and uncompromising as a preacher-man grappling with mortal sin.

'I'll handle my duties and my friendships as I see fit. Good day to you, sir.'

Carson stood, rock jaw thrusting. 'And you're a fool. You've still got some reputation left, but it's sinking fast. Mantee is a murdering butcher as he proved yet again out at the mine today. Yet you let him walk beside you and act like a deputy against men whose only crime is that they want a fair shake. And they deserve it.'

'Take my advice and quit my town, Carson. You're a troublemaker with ideas above yourself that could cost you dearly.' A calculated pause, then: 'Are you still here?'

Carson made to go, then paused.

'Have you ever thought it might be time, Sheriff?'

Hart paled. 'Time? Time for what?'

'To consider stepping down, of course. I've no doubt you're an honest honorable man, but a job this size and the troubles you've been having, well — '

'Get out! And keep out of my affairs or by God I'll . . . '

Carson didn't hear the rest.

As he quit the building a tall figure was approaching across the street. They saw one another at the same moment, Mantee immediately slowing his pace and narrowing his eyes. But Carson's reaction was more dramatic. He hauled his right-hand Colt in one lightning motion, jumped down in to the dust and rammed the piece into the startled man's solar plexus.

'You son of a bitch!' he hissed as citizens scattered wildly. 'You murdered Ethan and you murdered that man out at the mine today. Well, hear this good. You back off and leave the miners to Hart, or next time when I draw on you I'll gun you down like the dog you are!'

Mantee smirked as he lifted both hands and laughed mockingly.

'Hey, you've made your point, hero. I was always taught never to argue with a man who's holding a gun in your belly.'

A hundred pairs of staring eyes were upon Carson as he slowly housed the .45 and glanced back over his shoulder. The sheriff stood upon the porch, tall and straight with feet wide-planted and both hands resting on the scrolled leather of his heavy-laden gunbelt.

A line had been drawn in the sand from which it seemed that three strong men, so similar yet so different, might not be able to retreat.

Mantee and Carson continued to stand motionless as though locked together by their enmity, each seemingly ready to gunfight, yet each unwilling to begin it. And in that silence the street heard the rising sounds of racing horses and wild cries coming from the Copper King Road. Then a hysterical scream split the air.

'Scavengers!'

★　★　★

Forty miners had remained at the Copper King mine that day, despite its having been closed down following the accident and the riot. Holte Fort had insisted upon it. His intention was to give the town time fully to comprehend what had happened, then seek one last meeting with Coster Daley in the slender hope of hammering out a solution to their problems before the roof caved in. Fort had not defined what might occur should this latest mine collapse and yet another killing by Mantee fail to convince the copper boss that he must sit down and discuss terms.

But before the arrival of the rider from town the mobs had had time — far too much time in reality — to hash and rehash events and make their own violent decisions upon what should be done.

Whiskey and rum had fuelled their discussions, helping rough working men shed their inculcated fear of mine-guards and town-tamers to a point where they had become well and truly cogged into rebellion mode, long before their fellow-miner rode in on a long-eared mule now to report that Carson's attempt to set up a peace parley had just fallen through.

A hulking Cousin Jack kicked an empty bottle halfway across the mine yard. Another ran after it, picked it up and hurled it with unerring accuracy through a window of the administration block. Nervous guards came running, their sudden appearance goading the overheated mob into touching off a forward rush, angry voices lifting and roaring with animal-like depth and volume. The guards retreated back inside and crossbarred the doors.

It was at that moment that a ginger-headed miner in big heavy boots touched a match to an oil-soaked brand leaning against the tool-shed, grabbed it up and went running towards the mouth of the mine.

He never made it.

From the south side of the mine,

where pyramids of tailings climbed as high as thirty feet, the bellowing voice of Coster Daley suddenly sounded, flowing out over the attackers and defenders, causing them to halt in their tracks.

'Earn your money, scum!'

Scum? What scum? What money?

They weren't left long to wonder as forty wild-haired desert horsemen astride unshod maverick ponies exploded into view, screaming like banshees and firing into the miner's ranks at point-blank range.

★ ★ ★

It was like spontaneous combustion.

The miners in town were unaware of the murderous situation exploding out at the Copper King at that moment when the man whose brother had been killed by Mantee that morning walked out of the West Street gunshop with a pistol in hand and just began shooting.

A block west along the Boardwalk

stood a cluster of clapboard buildings housing office and administration staff of the mine and their families. Within moments of the gunshots erupting uptown, figures in miners' blue were running through the block, busting windows and smashing fences before converging on the Gunsight saloon where they were met by enraged towners. Battle was joined. The saloon mirror seemed to explode when a hurled bottle struck and a wild brawl erupted on the staircase, which soon began to give way beneath the press of bodies.

Outside on the street, Hart and Mantee were riding for the saloon when they encountered a dazed and bloody-faced miner astride a lathered horse, bearing the sketchy tidings of some unidentified disaster out at the Copper King mine.

The sheriff had no option. The King was Sundown's life-blood and his duty lay out there. After quickly mustering a posse he led his riders out at the gallop, making a decision that was more difficult for him than anyone could possibly know. He assigned to Mantee the task of quelling the riot. He was the only man capable, the only man willing. But he was the wrong man.

★ ★ ★

By the time Mantee came storming back down the Broadway the riot at the Gunsight had petered out, surprisingly without any loss of life. But already the infection of violence had spread to the main street where he saw miners running in and out of the general store in a looting orgy, while a full-scale eruption was spilling untidily across the gallery of the Buckhorn Hotel opposite. A terrified woman ran between two buildings with a miner clutching a bottle in laughing pursuit. Mantee's gun filled his fist as he dragged his horse to a long, sliding halt. He levelled the piece at shoulder-height and fired just the once. The running man's momentum kept him running on lifeless legs until he crashed headlong into a fire barrel, dead before he hit ground.

A rifle snarled from across the street and Mantee felt the hot sting of a bullet kiss his shoulder. He whirled. Several miners were emerging from an alley, most toting looted goods, just one with a rifle.

The big man's eyes changed color as he lifted his gun. Fanning the hammer, he chopped the rifleman down and kept shooting until there were five men down in the dust, writhing and screaming.

Moments before it had seemed that nothing could put the lid on the outbreak, yet this outpouring of blood appeared to achieve it in mere moments. Suddenly this no longer seemed like a justifiable riot. Hell! it was just bloody slaughter! Good men were dead and dying, and as Broadway slowed, paused and stopped to stare, they saw Mantee reloading calmly as he kneed his horse in the direction of the general store, where every man in blue appeared suddenly and frighteningly to be exposed.

He triggered without appearing to take aim and a man tumbled backwards dropping a tin of biscuits which broke open and spilled its contents in the dust. The sounds of wild panic as men tried to dash for cover almost drowned out the shout from the hotel: 'Enough, damn you!'

The man with the smoking gun whirled, a sick kind of excitement flooding his face when he sighted Carson's athletic figure leaping down the steps. 'Perfect!' he hissed. And to make it even better, there was Julia out on the gallery to see it all unfold.

Eagerly Mantee sprang to ground and housed his Colts. He would do this thing before her and the whole town in a way that none would ever forget. He would do it hero style.

'Are you interfering with the work of the law, drifter?' he shouted, flicking his hat from his head and flexing powerful shoulders. 'Please, admit you are.'

'I said enough!' Carson had halted, hands at his waist. 'These men are wrong but you're more wrong. I'm taking those guns off you, Mantee.'

'Better than that, I'll give them to you!'

Julia's horrified scream mingled with the deep-throated voices of the six-guns as two fast men came clear and fought it out at a range so close that billowing clouds of gunsmoke quickly shrouded them both. Mantee knew he was unbeatable with the Colts, believed it right up to the moment when white-hot death impaled him on a lance of invisible fire. He jerked his triggers once more, unaimed, their sound lost in a totality of final sound that seemed to engulf him as he staggered towards the dim figure of Carson, who stood tall and unmoving with smoking guns angled downwards now.

He crashed forward into the dust, silver hair still immaculate as his Stetson rolled away. He tried to speak but choked on blood. And in the great hush that followed, every citizen, chastened brawler and bystander stared fixedly with the same thought. That this had to mean the end of it, yet knowing it really wasn't. Not yet.

Hoofbeats.

★   ★   ★

'Eeeeeeyahhhh!'

The wild scream of the Scavenger riders at first seemed to have the desired effect which was to freeze the whole street with a primitive terror of the unknown, enabling the killers to begin the slaughter before they properly recovered.

It would surely have achieved the complete capitulation of the miners but for two men standing on opposite sides of the street. Two men who reacted swiftly like the professionals they were, as only professionals might.

The sheriff's first bullet cut down the howling head man, Mawby, and an instant later Carson snatched up Mantee's dropped pistols to pour a withering hail of lead into the exposed flanks of the horsemen as they stormed by. In mere moments the central block was littered with dead and dying figures.

Carson was turning corpses over in search of loaded guns when he realized that the street was again filled with a hailstorm of whistling death, with bullets on the wing whipping overhead, slamming into living flesh and bone, bringing men and riders down in a renewed orgy of blood.

He dived for the protection of a dead pony, then raised his head to see Sundown's long-suffering man in the street regain his manhood at the vital eleventh hour to fight back for his life, his town and his pride. The long-abused citizens of this hard-luck desert town were at this crucial moment goaded into rising up and fighting for themselves as they came swarming from every direction with guns in hand, and using them in their righteous wrath.

To triumph in that murderous fight.

* * *

Sheriff Hart stood in the shadowy gloom of the undertaker's parlor and lifted the white sheet from Mantee's dead face. Along at the Big Dipper, miners and townsmen, painted women and homey wives sat talking quietly while bartenders rested on their elbows. Nobody was drinking. Drink and rage and something primitive and unidentifiable had been let loose in the streets of Sundown that day, and now the whole town had fallen quiet, chastened and apprehensive.

This unnatural quietness permeated the hospital where hurt men lay in pain, wondering where their ministering angels had gone. An exhausted Ava Pearl and Julia Lee sat behind the smashed windows of the Squat and Gobble amongst the scattered glass, occasionally breaking off their conversation to

244

glance towards the back room where three men spoke behind closed doors.

At close quarters, mine-boss Daley was revealed as just an ordinary-looking little man turned gray and shaken by the events of a seemingly endless day. Time and time again in recent months he had been challenged, begged and threatened to do something about conditions at the Copper King, but it had taken a day like today, with dead and injured on all sides and the King barely saved from destruction by the marshal's posse, to wreak the change nothing else had been able to bring about before. The tycoon was speaking and Shane Carson and Holte Fort were listening, the miner's leader intent, the covert lawman with one ear cocked to the street, from where eventually, inevitably, a shout rang out with the ominous plangency of a brazen bell.

'Shane Carson, this is the sheriff!'

Daley fell silent and Holte grabbed for Carson's arm. 'No!' the man said. But Carson pulled loose, picked up his hat and went out through the diner. 'Forget it,' he said harshly with a curt gesture as the two women sprang to their feet. 'We all know it has to be done, so I'll do it.'

But Julia refused to allow him to go so easily, moving swiftly to block his way to the doors. 'This is foolish, Shane. It is just pride or vanity or some stupid code. The sheriff doesn't have to avenge Mantee's death, and you don't have to respond to his challenge. Please don't. I love you, Shane.'

He thrust past her and went out through the doors and into the street. Hart stood there exactly as Carson had pictured he might, the tall and commanding figure all in brown with low sunlight cutting across his somber face and twin guns snug in their holsters.

Shane squared his shoulders and walked slowly towards him.

'You killed Duke, Carson. I'm placing you under arrest.'

'It was self-defence, as you know. But you are bound and determined to come against me for it, so do it. Just don't try and make it sound legal or right, as it's neither.'

The Broadway held its breath for what seemed an eternity, expecting every passing second to usher in the shoot-out. A murmur swept the street and Carson heard steps and voices behind him but dared not turn. The lawman went white as he said: 'Ava, just what the hell do you think you are doing?'

Carson shot a sideways glance as the procession went by him, Ava, Julia, Holt — and Coster Daley. It was the Copper King boss who spoke first when the party interposed itself directly between the facing adversaries.

'You don't have to carry this foolishness through, Sheriff,' he declared in a voice that carried. He rested a hand on the lawman's shoulder. 'Today things went too far, shocked us both. But you see, as a result, I am agreeing to spend ten thousand to shore up the number three shaft and then . . . '

The cheering that drowned him out

came from the miners along the street but was quickly taken up by the towners. As Carson glanced both ways the lawman tugged at his jacket lapel and glared uncertainly at his lover.

'Damn you, Ava, this is man's business and you have no right — '

'How often have I seen you like this, Jack?' Ava said spiritedly. 'There's always a reason to fight but never a reason to stop. But don't you see? You've spoken to me unendingly about your determination to pacify this place, which you would eventually do — once enough men were in their graves. But we both know Duke was the real trouble here — '

'Ava, I — ' the haggard peace officer began, but she had the floor and was not about to relinquish it.

'You brought that gunman down here because you knew the job had grown too much for you, but you were too proud to admit it. Then you felt an obligation towards him that was mis-placed, when he went too far. Now he's dead and you want to turn on Shane, who is almost as bound up in a man's foolish code of honor as yourself. But don't you see? You both want the same thing, and it's being offered to you on a platter. Peace is at hand. All you must do now is set your male pride and vanity aside see what the town wants . . . what Julia and I want more than anything . . . '

There were tears in her eyes. Julia's eyes were full also as she stood with hands clasped before her, staring beseechingly at Shane Carson.

But Carson was studying the lawman intently and actually saw the rightness, the logic and the sheer common sense as it struck Jack Hart almost like a physical blow.

The lawman staggered and the street held its breath.

In an instant the iron sheriff appeared suddenly to shrink, to stagger a little, passing a hand over his eyes, then allowing Ava to rush to his side and support him when it appeared he might fall.

And in the moment when he glimpsed the lawman's gray face, Shane instantly knew and understood what was happening. For how long ageing Jack Hart had been gearing himself up, day after worsening day, in order to do the job he'd once done so easily, there was no telling. But this long day of blood had finally revealed his age and his secrets. He'd commanded the hell streets of the West for two decades, but never would again.

Carson himself had not fully escaped. He knew he could still do what he was paid for — visit trouble spots incognito at the behest of the Rosalee County Secret Bureau of Law — and pitch in to help set a town back on to the path of lawful revival and strength. But did this man wish to go on accepting the most difficult and dangerous assignments on a lawman's ledger?

He drew a shuddering breath and felt something slipping away from him, something that suddenly left him open to the possibilities of the new which he sensed might somehow be on offer here in this blood-soaked city of the desert, no matter how briefly.

Could Sundown change? Could the 'peacemaker with a .45' also change?

His eyes drilled questioningly at the lawman for interminable seconds as though seeking reassurance there. Until at last Hart nodded, sucked in a deep breath.

'I do believe they have a point, Carson.' A lengthy pause. 'These women we love, I mean.'

That word 'love' did it. All the iron tensions left Carson's sweat-streaked face and he was moving forward, right hand outstretched. The cheering began, uncertain and ragged at first, then stronger and far louder than before as two strong hands met and clasped over the body of a miner who had not, unlike them, lived to see the promise of a hard-won peace rise from the ashes of this mining town.

★ ★ ★

Two days later Shane Carson emerged from the Council Chambers weary, worn but exhilarated by what had been achieved. The war was over, past sins had been absolved, warring parties had realized that they'd had enough and had pledged their commitment to getting Sundown back on its feet and keeping it there. But what now for Shane Carson? he mused as he paused to study the poster advertising the vacant position of sheriff.

Until a voice sounded behind him: 'Officer Carson?'

He whirled, staring into the strong, suntanned face of fellow Headquarters operative Clancy Deakin from Rosalee County.

'What the hell . . . ?' he began. 'What are you doing here, man? I wired headquarters after I asked to be replaced to tell them that I'd changed my mind.'

'Guess I'd left by the time your wire got there,' the agent replied. He glanced around. 'Anyway, from what I see here, looks like they might need some extra help.'

'They do!' Carson said, his face lighting with sudden inspiration. 'We're going to need a mediator hereabouts for some time . . . and we sure as hell need a sheriff!'

'Huh?' the man said, uncomprehending.

'You peacemaker, me sheriff!' a grinning Carson said like a gruff Indian. He whirled and ripped down the poster, jabbed the frowning agent in the ribs. 'I'll explain later. Right now, you're in charge — Mr Mediator!'

He headed off at a run for the jailhouse, leaving Deakin staring after him. Then the Headquarters man half-grinned and wandered off in search for somebody who might be able to tell him what the hell was going on in this man's town.

We do hope that you have enjoyed reading this large print book.

Did you know that all of our titles are available for purchase?

We publish a wide range of high quality large print books including:
Romances, Mysteries, Classics
General Fiction
Non Fiction and Westerns

Special interest titles available in large print are:
The Little Oxford Dictionary
Music Book, Song Book
Hymn Book, Service Book

Also available from us courtesy of Oxford University Press:
Young Readers' Dictionary
(large print edition)
Young Readers' Thesaurus
(large print edition)

For further information or a free brochure, please contact us at:
Ulverscroft Large Print Books Ltd.,
The Green, Bradgate Road, Anstey,
Leicester, LE7 7FU, England.
Tel: (00 44) **0116 236 4325**
Fax: (00 44) **0116 234 0205**

THE BONANZA TRAIL

John Dyson

Dawson City was a rumbustious boom-town where whisky and champagne flowed. Men lost fortunes on the throw of a dice as thousands of greenhorns flocked into the Yukon's golden triangle. Hunter and guide Scope Mitchell was better equipped than most to survive the perils of the wilderness, but he had a battle on his hands when Frenchie Pete and his gang of thugs began stalking him. Would his lone rifle be a match for the outlaws?

THE BLOOD OF IRON EYES

Rory Black

In Arizona territory, bounty hunter Iron Eyes adds another outlaw to his tally and heads for the town of Hope to collect his reward money. Unfortunately, the outlaw had worked for Brewster Fontaine, who pretty much owns the whole town — including the bank . . . Fontaine orders his hired guns to kill Iron Eyes the moment he leaves the bank. But Iron Eyes is no ordinary bounty hunter and will wage war no matter how many guns he must face.

THE SHADOW OF THE GALLOWS

Steven Gray

When homesteader Ralph Bannister is murdered, Tom Steadman becomes the obvious suspect. After being found guilty and sentenced to be hanged, he seeks the help of Bellington's Private Detective Agency. Zachary Cobb and Neil Travis make the journey to Newberry — with only four days left to prove Steadman innocent. But Cobb's troubles begin before he and Neil even arrive in the town . . . It will take a great deal of blood and trouble before Bannister's real killer can be revealed.